NOT SLEEPING, JUST DEAD

JOE GOODEY MYSTERIES (BOOK 2)

CHARLES ALVERSON

WATCHFIRE
PRESS

Published by Watchfire Press.

Watchfire Press

www.watchfirepress.com

www.watchfirepress.com/alverson

Cover design by Kit Foster

www.kitfosterdesign.com

Not Sleeping, Just Dead/Charles Alverson. — 1st ed.

Print ISBN: 978-1-940708-27-0

ISBN: 9781940708263

ALSO BY CHARLES ALVERSON

Caleb

The Word

Goodey's Last Stand (A Joe Goodey Mystery)

Not Sleeping, Just Dead (A Joe Goodey Mystery)

Fighting Back

Mad Dog Brewster

Apache Dreaming

Imagine Me

Hooligans

The Triple Shot Box (3 Crime Novels)

The Coming of Age Box (3 YA Novels)

For a current list of titles and further information, please visit watchfirepress.com/alverson.

GET A FREE SHORT STORY COLLECTION

To instantly download ***Ryan's Way and Other Stories*** completely for free, sign-up for Charles Alverson's author newsletter at watchfirepress.com/alverson.

1

I WAS STRETCHING A TALL GIN AND TONIC AT ALDO'S, the only bar I knew that hadn't yet torn up my tab, when I looked up and discovered that my elbow room to the west had been annexed by an elderly gentleman in a three-piece suit.

Before I could decide how I felt about that, my new neighbor reached over and placed a cellophane-covered card over the mouth of my glass. Even in the dim light Aldo cultivated—he claimed that it confused germs—I could see that it was a business card identifying Frederick M. Crenshaw, Chairman, Cosmopolitan Fire & Casualty Insurance Co., Los Angeles. I had to make a quick decision: say something or drink the card.

"You're out of luck," I said. "Even if I bought some, someone would probably burn me down before the night was out."

He didn't answer but just flipped the card over, revealing a colored photograph of a fresh-faced girl with a wide mouth, freckles and long, auburn hair. She was wearing a white graduation gown and a mortarboard at a slightly rakish angle.

"Very pretty," I said, "but is she old enough to hang out in a joint like this?"

"She would have been," he said, withdrawing the photograph, "but she's dead now. She was my granddaughter."

"I'm sorry," I said automatically.

"Don't be," he said, slightly sharply. "It won't help Katharine or me. But you could help me a lot, Mr. Goodey, by finding out who killed her."

I sipped the watery dregs of my drink. "Do you want to tell me about it, Mr. Crenshaw?"

"Do you have an office?"

"Not one that I'm very eager to go back to right at this moment," I said honestly, if enigmatically. That's the trouble with having an office. I'd found in the nine months since I'd left the San Francisco Police Department that it gave people I didn't want to see very much—like Gabriel Fong and other creditors—a pretty fair idea where to find me.

"Well, then," said Crenshaw, still game, "have you had dinner?"

Yes," I said. "Quite often in the past. But not recently."

Twenty minutes of silent taxi ride later, we were putting our feet under an expensive tablecloth in a very private back room at McGinty's, the best steak house in San Francisco. Carlo, the waiter, an ectomorphic Italian with the eyes of a failed tenor, watched glumly as I ripped through the menu. A closet vegetarian, Carlo worried about my carbohydrate intake. He cheered up at Crenshaw's order of a bowl of clear broth and then disappeared through the thick velour drapes that separated us from the rabble.

I lapped appreciatively at some very nice claret and waited for Crenshaw to enlighten me further, but he didn't seem to be in an awful hurry. He took a drink from a glass of iced Perrier water and watched me with eyes that were not particularly kindly. Probably nobody at Cosmopolitan Insurance called him Uncle Fred. Crenshaw was a trim, upright man barely on the wrong side of sixty-five with a faintly military look that seemed cultivated. His cropped hair was an honest, uniform gray, which cast a pallor over regular but thin features. His eyes were a brittle blue and didn't seem to spend a lot of time twinkling. His well-kept hands had probably never touched anything dirtier than money.

Crenshaw seemed to be looking me over, too, possibly with a view to adopting me. I couldn't tell whether he liked what he saw, and I didn't care much. I'll eat any man's steak —friend or foe. Finally, he spoke.

"You're probably wondering, Mr. Goodey, how I know who you are and how I came to seek you out."

"The question occurred to me," I said, "but I imagine you'll tell me when you're ready."

His expression didn't change, but I could tell that he wasn't really too happy with my attitude.

"*If* you're going to work for me, Mr. Goodey," he said, "it is essential that we establish a viable relationship. Do I detect a certain negativity?"

I could guess that the sort of relationship he was thinking of wouldn't involve a lot of camaraderie. "Not really, Mr. Crenshaw," I said. "It's just that I'm hungry. I get a lot more likable with a full stomach."

At that moment, Carlo wafted in through the drapes and put a lobster bisque in front of me as if it were a time bomb. He lingered while I took my first taste, supposedly to see if I liked it, but I knew that he was waiting to see if I was *really* going to subject my insides to that sort of abuse. "Wonderful," I said with a glutton's smile. He administered the Kiss of Death with his black-olive eyes and disappeared.

Crenshaw thought he'd try again. "Ralph Lehman tells me that you've been off the police force since last August." So it was Ralph's size-nine sombrero from which Crenshaw had picked my name. Good old Ralph. He looked out for his boys even from beyond the veil of retirement. I knew Crenshaw must have been pretty desperate, or Ralph would never have put him onto me. Ralph loves me, I know, but he has no illusions that I'm Bulldog Drummond.

"That's right," I said, "but it hardly seems that long, I've been having such a good time."

His face pretended to believe me, but his eyes didn't bother. "Ralph was under the impression that life for a newly established private detective in San Francisco was somewhat—*straitened*," he said. I appreciated his nice choice of adjectives. He could have said poverty-stricken.

"I won't say I'm being measured for a yacht yet," I said, "but I've turned down more cases than I've accepted."

I skipped the details of those rejected cases. For instance, the one just that week in which a perfectly respectable car dealer had wanted me to kidnap his ex-wife and knock out all her teeth. They'd been really rotten when he'd picked the tramp out of the gutter, he said. Now she kept flashing them at him when they met in public. I had to refer him elsewhere.

And that overlooked the *really* unpromising offers I'd had since I'd turned in my shield for a private operative's license and a used hair shirt. But I didn't want to take the chance of depressing Crenshaw so much that he ran off before paying the bill. McGinty had a couple of lads in the back room who were expert at handling slow payers.

Carlo picked that moment to arrive, bearing about half of a charred cow and a disgusted expression. For the next little while I was too busy to do much talking anyway, so a discreet little silence, broken only by grunts from my side and the gentle lapping of the broth in Crenshaw's bowl, fell over the table. I couldn't help admiring his way with a soup-spoon. Each spoonful rose what seemed to be about four hundred feet from bowl to thin-lipped mouth with unerring precision and zero fallout. His back was parade-ground stiff, the eyes resting comfortably on the middle distance.

Once Crenshaw had reduced the broth to a polite level of about three sixteenths of an inch—without unseemly bowl-tipping—he placed his spoon at parade rest and patted spotless lips with the spotless linen napkin. "I hope you don't mind, Mr. Goodey," he said, "if I give you the background of the—situation—while you go on with your meal."

Caught in mid-chew, all I could do was bobble my head up and down. I could have used a bit more butter for my baked potato, but it didn't seem fair to make Crenshaw wait any longer. And I knew that Carlo would get after me about taking in too much cholesterol.

Crenshaw correctly interpreted my mime and began: "Mr. Goodey, are you familiar with an organization called The Institute?"

I nodded, choking only a little, and managed: "I've heard of it. But all I know is that it's some kind of cult down below Monterey that seems to have some problems with the neighbors and the authorities from time to time." I could tell from his expression that I hadn't exactly put The Institute in a nutshell, but he plowed on. "Last summer, Mr. Goodey, my granddaughter, Katharine Pierce, joined The Institute at its headquarters at Las Palomas near Big Sur. Katharine—her friends called her Katie"—he said this as if it were a mystery—"was a *restless* young girl. She quit Stanford University and had had a certain problem with—"

I could see that he was a bit stuck, so I swallowed the last of my steak and said: "Drugs?" It was a bit of a guess, but not that great considering what I knew of The Institute.

"Barbiturates, Mr. Goodey," he said, in case I was mentally bunching her with hash heads and needle enthusiasts. "Originally prescribed for her nerves. Unfortunately, Katharine became somewhat dependent on them. It was nothing really serious, but the doctors couldn't seem to help her." He paused. "Nor could I." That was probably as close to a confession as I was going to get out of Fred Crenshaw. "Then, early last summer, she went to a lecture given by a man called Hugo Fischer, the founder and president of The Institute. I don't quite understand what happened, but within days, Katharine had left her apartment on Nob Hill and had moved into The Institute's mansion at Las Palomas, taking a certain amount of money with her. Fortunately, most of her inheritance was legally tied up, but—"

Crenshaw suddenly realized that he was getting off on a tangent. Looking about as embarrassed as his nature would allow, he finished starkly: "On a Sunday morning late last December, Katharine was found dead on the rocks below the mansion. She had *allegedly* fallen from a roof terrace during the night." He leaned on the word *allegedly* so hard that it nearly snapped. And he wasn't too happy with *fallen*.

"At The Institute," he went on, "they claim that Katharine jumped to her death. I don't believe it. I want you to go down there and find out exactly what did happen. Will you do it?"

I didn't say anything right away. There was something

boiling behind his cool exterior, and I wanted just a peek at it. Even a dead-broke private investigator likes to get a glimpse of the real person who's hiring him. I took longer than was strictly necessary polishing off the claret and then spoke slowly.

"You think someone may have pushed your grand-daughter to her death from that terrace, Mr. Crenshaw." I didn't ask him; I told him.

Crenshaw's eyes, never jolly, took on a glittering hard-ness. He put a well-manicured hand on either side of his soup bowl; the knuckles were dead white.

"Mr. Goodey," he said with tightly reined vehemence, "I *know* that someone at The Institute injected my grand-daughter with a heavy dose of barbiturates and then threw her to her death on the rocks below. I want you to find out just who did it and see that they are punished. Will you do it?"

There was only one answer to that question, and I gave it. Crenshaw went back to being an aging, none-too-healthy business executive with a big problem. He put his hands back in his lap and asked me if I'd have any dessert. I almost said yes, but then decided that I couldn't face Carlo's disap-proving eyes.

Instead, we talked a bit more, and Crenshaw gave me three things: a check for a retainer big enough to let me hold my head up among my fellow men and my creditors; a thin, blue-folder report marked: "Confidential—Monterey County Sheriff's Department"; and another thicker report from an outfit called Brazewell Associates, Beverly Hills, California.

We agreed that I'd get in touch with him in Los Angeles just as soon as I had anything to report. To nobody's surprise, Carlo gave the bill directly to Crenshaw. Outside

McGinty's, Crenshaw favored me with a crisp handshake, advised me that he was staying at the Fairmont Hotel, and vanished in a taxi, leaving me standing there with only two problems in the world: getting used to having money in my pocket again, and finding out who—if anyone—had killed Katie Pierce.

2

My old friend and former boss, Ralph C. Lehman, newly retired as chief of detectives of the San Francisco Police Department, lived at the top of a modest hill in the not so sleepy little town of Mill Valley. When Ralph had moved in about thirty years before, Mill Valley had been so small and homey that the chief of police had come around personally to investigate the rumor that the new residents were of the Jewish persuasion. The Negro had not yet been invented in Marin County. Ralph had offered to dropkick the chief all the way to Milpitas and had lived there peacefully ever since.

I put my tired old Morris convertible into a tight turn up Molino Avenue and listened attentively for the first sounds of the death rattle. But the old four-banger took the challenge and somehow propelled me up Ralph's steep drive and onto the gravel apron in front of his crumbling Victorian house. Ralph came out onto the porch with a look of vexation on his big, ellipsoidal face. He was waving a sheet of white paper as if it were a flag of surrender.

He stepped all over my "Hi, Ralph" by booming: "Do

you know what those sons of bitches have done, Joe? They've nearly doubled the property taxes on this shack. I can't afford to live here anymore. They're going to drive everybody but the fags and the millionaires right out of Mill Valley."

I had a mental image of Mary Frances Lehman upstairs tying up a bundle of rags for the trip to the poorhouse, but then there she was peering out at me through the half-open screen door.

"Oh, shut up, Ralph," she said. "Stop rending your garments for a moment and make us a drink. Come on in, Joe. He's going to do the heath speech from *King Lear* in a minute, and I want to be sure to miss it."

I followed the tight bun at the nape of Fran's neck into the Lehman's big, old-fashioned living room. In one corner, Ralph's small desk overflowed with bills and receipts. In another, a television set flickered soundlessly as a black dude in a malnourished afro stretched his mouth and gesticulated at us. The room smelled of well-waxed wood and old leather and softly gleamed with brass and copper ornaments.

Ralph went over to a mahogany drinks cabinet and began rattling bottles while Fran whirled and leveled a long, bony finger at me. "You haven't been to see me in months," she accused. "All you have to do is retire, and all your friends pretend you're dead."

Before I could defend myself, Ralph forced a cold glass into my hand and fell into his massive, green leather chair at one side of the big stone fireplace in which a small fire behaved itself.

"Mary was up here with her sniveling little brutes last week," Fran continued. "She sends you her love, but she wasn't surprised to hear that you'd gone wrong."

I'd first met Fran Lehman as a hot-blooded claimant for her daughter Mary's hand about a dozen years before when I'd been a young detective just out of the blocky, blue uniform of the SFPD. Mary had wisely decided to marry a petrochemical engineer from Los Angeles, thus breaking my heart. And once I'd gotten past the gargoyle front Frannie put up, she'd become an auxiliary mother to me.

"You can tell your faithless daughter that I am risen from the fallen," I said, putting Crenshaw's check in front of Fran's face.

"Not bad," she said. "Who did you have to promise to kill? No, don't tell me. Then I can't tell the Grand Jury." She gathered up a wicker basket of embroidery and her drink. "I sense a certain amount of business talk coming up," she said, "and I'm too old and cantankerous to have to put up with it. You can find me in the nunnery."

Before the door quite closed behind her, I asked Ralph:

"This Crenshaw bird you've sicced onto me, how much do you know about him?"

Ralph communed with the ice cubes in his glass before saying: "Fred Crenshaw was the best defensive end I ever saw. Between us we ruined more halfbacks than you've had Chinese dinners. I used to slow them down, and Fred would break them off just below the knees. It was murder." He said this with gentle, contemplative relish as if remembering a great wine.

"I'll bet," I said. "But I assume that he's given up that habit by now. Do you think you could bring me up to date a bit?"

"He was in the war, you know," Ralph said, as if I hadn't spoken. "The Marines. Used to crawl into Japanese machine-gun nests and slit throats. Won a couple of medals that way."

"Thanks a lot, Ralph," I said. "I now know who killed his granddaughter. Crenshaw did, by crawling into her machine-gun nest, breaking her off at the knees and slitting her throat. Case closed."

"Don't look at me like that, Joe," he said, not sounding very hurt. "I'm not quite senile yet. Look at these eyes. Do you see any geriatric haze over them?"

I had to admit that I didn't. Any haziness would have been Scotch-induced, and I couldn't begrudge Ralph that.

"Well, then," Ralph said, "don't be too wise. I didn't ask you to come begging for information. Hell, I got you the job, and now you want me to carry you around piggyback. Remember, I was the one who advised you to take the mayor's offer of your old job back. You wanted to be a lousy private operative. So operate. If I'd wanted to handle this case, I'd have taken Crenshaw's money myself."

"All right," I admitted. "I'm lazy. And I'm a smart aleck. But you did put mad dog Crenshaw onto me, right? And you two seem to go back to the day before they invented fire. If I sit here like a good boy, do you think you could enlighten me about him? Just a little?"

Ralph sucked up a little more Scotch and looked relenting. "Okay," he said. "But don't interrupt. And try to look intelligent."

I nodded intelligently.

"Right," he said. "When Stanford University decided that it could do without my services as a mayhem artist, Fred stayed on to make All-American, Phi Beta Kappa, and to win a Rhodes Scholarship. Fred was a bit of a brain in those days. He came back, went into business and, except for that unpleasantness we called World War II, pursued a very successful career and made a few million dollars, most of which, if I know Fred, he still has."

"Is there a Mrs. Crenshaw?"

"There was," he said. "Just before the war he married a Miss Evelyn De Lane Ventnor of the Nob Hill, Palm Beach and Honolulu Ventnors. Evelyn was no great beauty, but she served to humanize Fred a bit and helped him several hundred rungs up the social ladder at the same time. In those days, Fred wanted to be a social lion. And she brought along a fair little slice of the Ventnor millions."

"A useful match," I said. "Since they had a grandchild, I'm assuming that Fred and Evelyn had at least one child."

"Just one," said Ralph. "A son, Fred Junior, but called Bud or something equally awful. Went off to Korea in a Sabre jet and came back in a bronze urn. The daughter-in-law gave birth to Katie about five months later, got remarried to a Nevada rancher named Pierce and took Katie to live there."

"And?" I said just to keep my vocal cords tuned up.

"Fred didn't see much of Katie for about ten years. Mrs. Junior didn't care much for his high-powered style. In the early sixties, Mr. and Mrs. Pierce split the blanket, and she took Katie to live in Las Vegas. Not long after, Evelyn died of something premature, painful and lingering, leaving a trust fund of about three million bucks."

"To?"

"Katie. The trust to become hers when she turned twenty-one."

"A useful sum," I said, "but unless I miss my guess, not to Katie anymore. Who was the lucky heir?"

"One guess," said Ralph, "but the initials are FMC, and you've met him. Not much later, Fred was struck down by an ungovernable hankering to have Katie by his side. I don't doubt that he did feel a belated resurgence of grandfatherly feeling, but if I know anything about Fred, the trust fund made him feel it all the keener."

"Highly understandable," I said. "Let me guess what happened next. Crenshaw went wading over to Nevada, slugged Mrs. Junior with an attractive lump sum and brought young Katie back to Los Angeles strapped to the pommel of his saddle."

"Close enough," Ralph said. "Katie was sent to all the best schools, put on all the cutest ponies and generally spoiled rotten. Fred bought her into Stanford, but it didn't do much to stop the rot. All she seemed to study was folk singing and pill popping, and the last couple of years she spent more time in clinics and shrinks' offices than at the university. So Stanford gave her the boot and probably cost themselves a million-dollar bequest. Katie went her way until she ended up at The Institute last summer. Fred didn't like it, but it seemed better than the street. I didn't hear any more until she took the big fall just before Christmas. Then I began to hear a lot more about her than I could stand."

"Fred figured you ought to do something."

"Not at first," Ralph said, crunching an ice cube. "Fred was perfectly happy to let the sheriff's office down in Monterey handle it as long as they came up with the right answer—his right answer—right away and no dillydallying. Unfortunately, they didn't, and that was when Fred started to lean on them. Until you've been leaned on by Frederick Melhuish Crenshaw, you haven't lived. You know Sheriff Dominguez?"

"The same way I know Governor Brown. I've seen his picture in the paper. Little Mexican fellow, isn't he?"

"Not exactly. To call Luis Dominguez a little Mexican is like describing Lorenzo de' Medici as a dead wop.

Dominguez is Spanish, so Spanish he makes your gums swell, and no touchier than the average fencing master."

"He and Fred didn't get along?"

"In a word: Not a fucking bit. Fred became such a nuisance that they nearly took out the phones. When he found out that even the Crenshaw millions couldn't make the sheriff's office roll over and play dead, Fred fell back on a high-powered—and higher-priced—firm of private investigators down in L.A."

"Brazewell Associates," I said.

"Those were the fellers. As you'll discover when you read their report, Brazewell's men got nowhere at The Institute. They were able to tell Fred a lot about that estimable organization and its founder that he didn't know, but they got no further than Dominguez's boys when it came to finding out how Katie Pierce came to die on those rocks. It's a lovely report—good syntax, neatly typed, attractively presented—but no good to Fred. He couldn't even wipe his butt with it. Fred gritted his teeth, paid through the nose, and—"

"Came running back up here to you."

"Yes. I read the sheriff's report, read Brazewell's very interesting document, shrugged my shapely shoulders and passed him on to you. End of story." Ralph settled back in the big leather chair as if that were true.

"Why me, Ralph?" I asked. "Sure, I can use the money. If anybody hates starving to death, it's Jonah Webster Goodey. And I know we're old friends, even if you did let them run me off the force last year just to collect your rotten pension. But what have I got that Dominguez and the Brazewell organization haven't?"

Ralph looked smug. "What you've got that they haven't, Joe boy, is a very good in with The Institute."

I don't mind being a straight man. "I'll bite," I said. "What would that be?"

"You know Rachel Schute," he said.

That was true enough. I did know the Widow Schute. And although I really liked Rachel and had spent the best part of a year doing a poor imitation of a gigolo, it hadn't been any good. After a few desultory attempts to meet her exalted expectations, I'd done a calculated drift out of her life last autumn and hadn't seen her for over six months. I'd heard no word of attempted suicide at her half-million-dollar tepee over in Sausalito.

"So what?" I said.

"So Rachel Schute is in very deep with The Institute, and from all reports seems to be getting in deeper by the minute. I hope it won't come as too big a shock, Joe, but she's even romantically involved with one of The Institute's big shots, some sort of doctor, I think."

That was a small surprise. I hadn't imagined that Rachel spent her nights knitting me bed socks, but I couldn't imagine what she was doing messing around with The Institute. She didn't even smoke pot.

"Some cynics," Lehman continued, "have been nasty enough to suggest that Hugo Fischer has his froggy eyes on Mrs. Schute's bulging moneybags. That's slander, of course, but all the same, it's pretty interesting."

"Sure, it's interesting. Several million bucks is always interesting. I wish Fischer a lot of luck. But what makes you think Rachel is going to make The Institute roll out the red carpet for me even if she does have some clout down there? You may not have heard over here in the sticks, but we're no longer an item. She gave me back my fraternity pin last fall."

"That's not the way I hear it," Ralph said. "I hear that

the Merry Widow still carries a modest torch for you, though only God knows why. You're not exactly Paul Newman. But if I were you and wanted to earn that impressive check you've been flaunting around here, I'd get over there and see how much credit you've got left with Mrs. Schute. You might be surprised. And I wouldn't be amazed if Hugo Fischer welcomed you if not with open arms, at least without setting the dogs on you."

3

It seemed pretty crass to use a dead romance as a lever to get inside The Institute. And if Rachel didn't think the romance was so extinct, that made it even worse. A guy would have to be pretty low to do that sort of thing.

Such thoughts occupied me all the way to Rachel's place in Sausalito. As I parked the old Morris in the carport and climbed the redwood steps to Rachel's front door, I was none too proud of myself. I'll bet my knock even had a shamefaced sound to it.

Ethelberta, Rachel's black maid, answered the door with a "What, you back again?" look on her somber face and left me standing deep in grass-colored carpet while she went to spread the good news and hide the best silver. Long before, Ethelberta and I had developed a symbiotic relationship. I didn't try to bullshit her, and she didn't sell me any tickets to the Black Panther's Ball. It wasn't much, but it was better than nothing.

Either there was more silver to hide these days or the news of my arrival hadn't been received in milady's chamber with much jubilation. I was beginning to feel like the second bride at a wedding. I studied the brushstrokes on an early Picasso, but time was beginning to get heavy on my hands when at last Rachel Schute came down the stairs with a less than welcoming expression on her face.

One glance at that face told me that I could have picked a better time for my visit. It was a face in transition from sleepy sensuality to a public expression of not particularly happy anticipation. I astonished myself by feeling a small surge of jealousy. She looked good, flushed slightly either from recent exertion or the knowledge that I could read her face pretty well. For the moment I felt some regret, which I did my best to smother.

"Hello, Joe," she said in her throaty voice. "I didn't expect you." I was trying to come up with a response when someone else came down the stairs behind Rachel.

He wasn't a big man, but he had a beefy, substantial look that made up for it and a square, slightly florid face with plenty of residual scowl lines. If he were a drunk, he'd be the nasty kind who always wants two olives in his martini and howls the "Yellow Rose of Texas" out of tune. But just then he wasn't drunk. He was mentally tucking in his shirttails and looking smug. I did not take an immediate liking to him.

Rachel looked nervously over her shoulder at him and said: "Joe, this is Dr. James Carey. Jim, this is Joe Goodey. I think I mentioned him."

I'd bet she had, but I didn't care to learn what she'd mentioned about me.

"Evening, doctor," I said brightly. "I didn't know you guys made house calls anymore." I turned to Rachel with a concerned expression on my face. "I hope none of the boys is ill."

Rachel couldn't decide whether I was being a smart ass,

but she decided to give me the benefit of the doubt. "Jim isn't that kind of doctor, Joe—I mean, he is, but he isn't practicing right now. He's a director of The Institute. You have heard of it, haven't you?"

From her tone of voice, I knew I was supposed to have, so I decided not to mess around. "I have, Rachel," I said. "That's what I've come to see you about. Do you think we could sit down for a minute?"

The idea startled Rachel a bit. She'd forgotten that we were standing there like actors frozen in position after the second-act curtain. "Of course," she said. "We'll have some coffee."

We settled comfortably on twin couches of pale green crushed velvet, with them facing me. A trenchant silence reigned while Ethelberta poured the coffee. "Thank you, Ethelberta," Rachel said. "Why don't you go home now?"

"All right, Mrs. Schute," she said. "Good night, doctor." Her eyes passed over me with all of the expression of twin fog lights, and Ethelberta headed for the door. I let her get her hand on the knob and then said "Ethelberta?" in a voice she couldn't safely ignore.

She pivoted warily and dropped her eyes on me.

"Nice to see you again," I said.

Her tea-colored face went even bleaker. "Thank you," she said flatly, pivoted again and moved smartly through the doorway, shutting the door crisply behind her.

Rachel didn't bother to comment on this little interplay, but came right to the point. "I don't understand, Joe. Why have you come to see me about The Institute?"

"It has to do with an assignment I've just taken on," I said. "Somebody wants me to find out who killed Katharine Pierce, the girl who died there last December. And I'd like you to help me get in there. I've heard—"

"No one killed Katie Pierce," Carey butted in. "She jumped or fell from the terrace, and that's that. There is no need for further investigation."

"You sure about that, doctor?" I asked.

"Yes, I am. And we don't need any more cheap private detectives prowling around wasting our time. That case is closed."

That was said positively enough. I wished that I was as sure of anything as he seemed to be about everything. I was about to beg to differ when Rachel saved me the trouble.

"What makes you so sure, Jim?" she asked, in a tone I knew all too well. Rachel has her soft moments, but she's no pushover. I knew—and Carey was no doubt beginning to realize—that he'd gone a bit far.

He brought his tone down a shade or two. "Hell, Rachel," he said, "you know that we've already had two investigations. First, the sheriff had his men all over the place, and then those slick characters from Los Angeles were nosing around for weeks. Don't you think that's enough?"

Worried that his reasoning might get to Rachel, I said: "Dr. Carey, a young girl—not yet twenty-one—has died under very suspicious circumstances. An old man wants to know just what happened to his only granddaughter. Do you think that's so very unreasonable?"

"Crenshaw knows, Goodey," Carey said, fighting a rear-guard action. "The sheriff's department told him. That ought to be good enough, even without those private detectives. Katie's death was an accident—or possibly suicide. She was a very mixed-up girl."

"She was a very doped-up girl when she went off that terrace, Dr. Carey," I said. "Is that usual at The Institute?"

"Of course not," he said. "You have no idea—"

"That's why I want to come to The Institute," I said, running right over him. "If only to satisfy her grandfather once and for all. That's not so much to ask, is it, Rachel?"

I thought I could count on Rachel feeling tender toward poor, dead Katie Pierce, and she didn't fail me. She turned to Carey with an expression half imploring and half demanding, something that seems to come easy to rich women.

"No, it's not. It's really not, Jim. I don't see what harm it can do if Joe can settle in the old man's mind what happened to that poor girl. It's not as if The Institute has anything to hide. Is it?"

"Of course not," he came right back on cue. He turned his pale eyes toward me challengingly. "Goodey," he started, "you can—" But then he thought of something. "Rachel," he asked, "may I use your telephone?"

While he was out in the hall doing just that, Rachel and I sat staring at each other. There didn't seem to be much to say. I learned that her three boys were just fine. She learned that I was staying alive but not getting rich.

Carey came back into the room looking more confident, even aggressive. I hoped he hadn't been drinking out there. "Goodey," he said, "you come on down to The Institute. Come any time. Turn the place upside down. Maybe you're right. Maybe this is the way to get that old nut off our backs for good."

"Would tomorrow be too soon?"

"Come right now," he challenged. "I'll drive you down myself."

"Thanks," I said, "but I can see that you're busy here, and I've got to wash a pair of socks. I'll come down tomorrow if that's okay. You'll be there, Rachel?"

"I was going to be there anyway," she said, "for a

wedding. But now that you're going, I wouldn't miss it for the world. I want to be around when you bump into Hugo."

"Yeah," I said. "Sounds like fun. See you then, Doctor?"

"Oh, sure," Carey said, but didn't sound all that sure. But it wouldn't do him any good to have doubts. I was going to The Institute, and with Rachel behind me, I might even have a chance of staying there long enough to learn something. If there was anything to learn.

I got up from the comfortable couch. "I won't keep you folks up any longer," I said. "Thanks very much for your time." Rachel's mouth tightened. That's not very good for the facial wrinkles when you're pushing forty-five, but I didn't think that was a good time to mention it.

I drifted into the hall, followed by Rachel with a mixed expression on her face. Dr. James Carey skulked in the drawing room doorway, looking baleful. He hadn't been very happy to see me and he didn't look sad to see me go. I have that effect on people sometimes.

As I went through the front door, I turned back toward Rachel. "It was good to see you again," I said. "You're looking fine, Rachel." And she was. There must be something about getting laid regularly that brings a high polish to a mature woman's appearance. "The Institute seems to be doing you good."

"It is, Joe," she said. "You could use some of what it has yourself."

"We'll see about that," I said. "It didn't seem to do a lot for Katie Pierce. See you tomorrow." I turned to walk down the stairs.

"Joe," she said quietly, and I stopped with my foot in midair. "Do you have to be such a *complete* bastard?" she asked just as quietly and closed the big door.

Rachel's question gave me something to think about as I

recrossed the Golden Gate Bridge and headed for North Beach. Maybe Rachel was right. Maybe I was jealous because somebody had picked up something I'd rejected. I wouldn't put it past me.

But before I could ponder the point to death, I was pulling off Broadway and heading into the little cul-de-sac where I lived at the tail end of Chinatown. It hadn't changed much since morning. The dingy, dun-colored apartment houses still huddled together in self-protective squalor. Lum Kee's grocery store lurked on the ground floor of my building, but it was run by a manager, an old lady with young eyes. Lum Kee, my late landlord, had gone to his ancestors with about four inches of war-surplus steel in his gut. I wondered what sort of celestial crooked deals he was working.

A man with money in his pocket must walk differently. Before I was halfway across the narrow street, I heard a familiar voice hailing me. "Hello, Joe," said Gabriel Fong, just by coincidence getting out of his red Jaguar parked at the curb.

"Hi, Gabe," I said innocently. "What a surprise to find you here. Come on up and have a drink."

Suspicion crossed his round young face, but he followed me up the narrow, threadbare stairs to my small apartment. At that hour, the cooking odors from the other apartments had faded a bit, but it was still the next best thing to eating a Chinese meal. And less fattening.

Opening my door, I kicked a pile of unpaid bills to one side. The musty, unlived-in smell of the place met me. I made a mental note to myself: Start living.

Gabriel Fong watched me silently while I poured out two glasses of Napa Valley red. He'd probably had something else in mind. Fong had changed a lot since I'd met him the summer before. Then he'd been a clean-cut Bible College student, all fuzzy and sincere and full of apparently genuine piety and good works. But something radical had happened to him since he'd taken over Uncle Lum's motley empire on the death of that old devil. He'd vowed he was going to run the enterprises for the greater glory of God. But lately, his two hundred dollar suits, Italian haircut and—especially—the red Jag indicated that Mammon might just be winning out. Gabriel's jaded eyes spoke of something a bit more secular than church socials.

"Drink this, Gabe," I said, giving him the wine. "You look as though you could use it."

"It's not an easy life, Joe," he said, lifting his weary head from the back of my old green couch. "The responsibilities of being a landlord are many and taxing. You wouldn't—"

"I would," I said. "Chasing tenants for the rent must be a real burden. I'll bet some of them are, as much as three months in arrears. I'll bet."

"Four," he said sadly. "One is four months overdue." I knew he wasn't just quoting a random statistic.

"Well, Gabe," I said, "I know you're not worried about my rent, but, just in case, have a look at this." I put Crenshaw's check into his plump hand.

Fong looked at it for a while, memorizing the sum, subtracting the amount I owed him and probably wondering how I was going to waste the rest of it. "Is that a genuine check, Joe?" he asked.

"It had better be," I said. "I don't mind so much for myself, but you probably need another Jaguar."

He let that pass. The check had him mesmerized. I fancied I could hear the whirr of tiny wheels and cogs. "This Frederick M. Crenshaw, Joe," he said at last, "would you say he was a substantial man?"

"Only the chairman of the Cosmopolitan Insurance Company," I answered. I was enjoying the prestige of my new association with Frederick M. Crenshaw.

Fong was impressed, but he didn't like to show it. He just blinked and said: "I'll cash it for you and give you the balance." He made it sound like a big favor. "After I deduct your rent."

"That's okay, Gabe," I said. "No need to bother. I'll put it in the bank and send you a check. I don't want to leave you short of pocket money."

"No problem, Joe," he said, pulling out a thick roll of bills. Faster than I could have counted my fingers, he'd done the calculation and peeled off a respectable number of bills. "Here," he said, as if giving me a prize. "Now your rent is paid. Just sign your regular signature on the back of the check, Joe."

I ignored the ballpoint pen he was shoving at me and slowly counted my share of Crenshaw's retainer. Even though I had failed algebra, my calculations told me that Fong had subtracted five months' rent. I held out my hand, palm up. Fong knew what I was getting at.

"It's to your own advantage, Joe," he said persuasively. "Think how secure you'll feel with your rent paid in advance."

"Think how terrible I'll feel if I get gored by a musk ox tomorrow and die knowing that I'd overpaid my rent. Give."

He did. Slowly, reluctantly, sorrowfully as if he were making a down payment on his own coffin. "Now beat it," I said, "while I start to earn some of that money I just paid you."

As Fong's light footsteps died on the stairs, I snapped on my gooseneck lamp and sat down at the table to study the documents Crenshaw had given me. The sheriff's report was simple and straightforward, a model of terseness and economy. It stated, in brief, that Katharine Melhuish Pierce, a Caucasian spinster twenty years old, had been found dead of head injuries on the rocks below The Institute (formerly known as the Carter mansion) on the morning of December 21, 1975. The fatal injuries were consistent with those that might be caused from such a fall, and the deceased had been dead for approximately eight hours when found.

The report went on to say that there was no evidence to indicate how Katie had come to fall from the roof terrace on top of the building. There were no known witnesses to the death, and the inmates—now, there was a word that the folks at The Institute wouldn't be crazy about—although cooperative with investigators, hadn't been able to shed any light on why Katie had been on the terrace or how she'd come to fall off.

The sheriff's report gave a bit of background on Katie, including the fact that she'd been at The Institute for just under six months, but most of it was the same information Crenshaw had given me at McGinty's. And it didn't miss the fact that the late Miss Pierce had had a high concentration of Phenobarbital in her blood stream when she died. In short, she was higher than a steeplejack's insurance premiums. That was worth thinking about. Supposedly, one of the great attractions of The Institute to Katie had been that it helped her lose her pill habit. Or perhaps lose was a bit strong. The cure didn't appear to have been all that permanent.

The neatly bound, professionally typed report from Brazewell Associates was written in better English and a lot more of it; Brazewell's boys certainly scored high for thoroughness. Crenshaw now knew more about The Institute and Hugo A. Fischer than he probably wanted to know.

What he wasn't any closer to knowing was who had killed his granddaughter. The Brazewell investigators, who also knew how to read an autopsy report, noted the phenobarb in Katie's blood and suggested in the most subtle way possible that she just might have imagined she was Amelia Earhart and tried to fly to Hawaii.

This was not a suggestion likely to appeal to old man Crenshaw, and the Brazewell Report tried to make up in solid, well-researched information what it may have lacked in originality. It took Hugo Amholdt Fischer right back to Lamar, Missouri, where in 1927 he had the good fortune to be born the third son of a dirt farmer whose sidelines were Bible thumping and gin swilling. The report followed Fischer through an undistinguished academic career that ended after the tenth grade and into sporadic employment as a merchant seaman. That is, when he wasn't in various Midwest slammers for such eccentricities as bad checks, assault and no visible means of support.

To telescope a lot more than Brazewell Associates felt able to do, Fischer was an amphibious bum for the first thirty-seven years of his life. Then in 1964, while working on a banana freighter in South America, he sampled one of the more exotic indigenous psychedelic substances. According to Fischer, he immediately experienced such a flash of insight that he jumped ship and caught the next plane to New York. To quote one of his fruitier declarations: "I instantly knew my destiny. I could visualize in broad outline the creation of a great social movement. All I had to do was make it happen."

Fischer flew into New York without even bus fare to Manhattan in his pocket and began a tough three or four years while he gathered followers. One stroke of luck, according to the report, was that this was the beginning of the flower-power era, and some of the flower children, in various stages of disintegration, began to flock to his banner.

But his Appeal wasn't limited to hippies. According to Brazewell, Fischer's little movement consisted of neurotics, psychotics, alcoholics, workaholics, nymphomaniacs, blocked writers, pill heads, middle-class dropouts, homosexuals, just plain crooks and hoodlums and even a few hard-drug addicts whom nobody else had been able to get off the needle. And from this rabble emerged The Institute of Mankind, later shortened to just The Institute.

According to the report, in 1965 Fischer married Lenore Harston, heiress to a small textile fortune and some-time mental patient, now forty-five years old. They had no surviving children, although a son, Hugo Junior, died shortly after his birth in 1967. For a time in 1973, Mrs. Fischer left The Institute, but she returned the next year.

The report went into some detail on Fischer's leading disciples, among whom was the following: "A quite recent recruit, as yet non-resident, is Mrs. Rachel Schute, forty-four, a widow and multi-millionairess of Sausalito, California. Mrs. Schute first visited The Institute's headquarters in January of this year and appears to have been quickly given the status of privileged guest. This would seem to be not unconnected with Mrs. Schute's considerable wealth, which she inherited on the accidental death of her late husband, Howard Schute in 1973. She has apparently developed a relationship with Dr. James Carey, an ex-alcoholic who is one of Fischer's top lieutenants. It would of course be libelous to suggest that The Institute is endeavoring to provide Mrs. Schute with a new husband in return for certain financial advantages."

It would indeed. Those Brazewell people walked a pretty fine line when it came to libel. I'd have liked to have seen Rachel's face when she read that passage. Or better yet, the good doctor's. If Fischer had his hooks out for a large hunk of Rachel's money, he'd better be fairly sharp. She was no fool where money was concerned.

There was a lot more to the report, but I'd had enough for the moment. I've never been one to do too much homework, anyway. It takes the edge off your ignorance. A careful study of the Brazewell Report would probably have told me who killed Katie Pierce, but where would be the fun in that?

Besides, something was bothering me. Something small but sharp and irritating was niggling at the back of my brain. Not about the Brazewell Report or even what I would find at The Institute. It had to do with Fred Crenshaw. I went over our conversations in my mind, and somehow something just didn't ring true. There was something missing. My watch told me that it was nearly midnight. Crenshaw was probably tucked snugly away by then, enjoying whatever kind of dreams millionaires have. On the other hand, he might not be able to sleep, either. It wouldn't hurt to go find out.

4

It was a fine spring night, so I decided to walk. The Morris could use the rest, and I needed the exercise. Jackson Street was almost empty, and except for an interesting offer hissed at me from a dark alley by a young girl—I think it was a girl—my walk was uneventful until I turned onto Powell Street and looked doubtfully up the steep back slope of Nob Hill toward the Fairmont Hotel.

My resolve to walk it was melted by the clang of the Powell Street cable car coming back from Fisherman's Wharf and the bellowing voice of my old buddy Rolly Poole: "Come on, Joe, if you're too cheap to pay, I'll give you a free ride." The car had stopped at the intersection, and I could see Rolly's massive shape among the tall levers in the dark interior of the driver's slot.

"Best offer I've had all night, Rolly," I said, jumping aboard the running board and getting a grip on a pole just over the head of a pretty Mexican girl. "How goes it?" I'd shared a squad car with Rolly in my early days on the force. Then he'd been a ten-year veteran on the verge of picking up sergeant's stripes. But without warning one night, I'd found that I had a new partner, and that Rolly had been arrested for beating a pimp to death on Russian Hill.

The call girl in the middle of the action showed her gratitude by turning state's witness, and Rolly picked up seven long ones over in San Quentin. However, his wife, Helen, kept the family together and never missed a visiting day. And when the parole board sprang him, Rolly found himself at the front of the long line for a job on the cable cars. The department takes care of its own, even when they've been a bit naughty. Now Rolly's woolly hair was shot with dapple gray, and a lot of muscle had turned to fat, but I still wouldn't have liked to get caught in the grip of his powerful arms on the levers.

"Couldn't be better, Joe," he said, giving the bell a bash and setting the car in motion. "You know my little Vanessa? She's going to be a rock and roll singer, and I'm going to retire to manage her. Only about twenty thousand more trips up this damned hill and I'm a free man."

The conductor, a slim, blond kid with a healthy crop of pimples, took a couple of fares but passed me by. A black guy carrying a big package snorted and told the night air. "Man, that's rich. These honkies sure do stick together. No fare or nothing." He snorted again.

"Joe's no honky, stud," Rolly told him, braking the car at Washington Street. "He's an albino. You ought to see him dance." That won him another snort. "You working, Joe?"

"You could call it that," I said. "I'm on my way up to the Fairmont to call an old man a liar." The girl in front of me, who'd been ignoring our conversation, looked disapproving.

"Nice work if you can get it," said Rolly, clanging the bell vigorously at a kamikaze on a big Honda. "You really going to stick to this private cop scam?"

"You got any better suggestions?" I asked him, half hoping that he did. But Rolly got busy with the levers, and by the time he'd finished slamming them about and cursing under his breath, he seemed to have forgotten the question, and the cable car was creeping up to the brow of Nob Hill at California Street. "See you, Rolly," I said, jumping off the still-moving car.

"Sure," he shouted. I was on the sidewalk at the back of the Fairmont Hotel when I heard him add: "Give him one for me." That was touching. Old cops never lose their instincts.

Crenshaw had told me his room number, so I went directly to the house phone in the nearly deserted lobby. The night man looked up at me with mild curiosity, but he didn't go for his gun or scream for help, so I must have looked fairly legitimate. The reluctant operator put me through to Crenshaw's room.

If I'd expected to confront a sleep-befuddled old man, I'd have been disappointed. Crenshaw's crisp "Hello. What do you want?" gave the impression that he'd been sitting bolt upright waiting for my call. He received the news that I wanted further words with him without warmth, but suggested that I come right up.

Before I could hit the door a second time, Crenshaw opened it. "Good evening, Mr. Goodey," he said and closed the door behind me. "Why have you come to see me so soon? Surely you haven't learned anything useful yet." That was businesslike enough, if a bit pessimistic about my ability. He was dressed in a rich but not gaudy silk dressing gown and still had his teeth in. The bed was West Point neat, and on a table near a standard lamp was an open book and a glass of what could have been whiskey and water. No bottle was in sight, and I didn't think I'd get offered a drink.

"Not very much, Mr. Crenshaw," I said, feeling sleepy and not in the mood for a lot of polite chatter. "Only that you haven't yet told me the real reason why you want me to find out who killed your granddaughter."

That got all his attention. Crenshaw turned his impassive eyes on me and asked: "You're not satisfied with my explanation, Mr. Goodey?" It was obvious that he wasn't used to taking lip from the hired hands. I sat down uninvited on a straight chair next to the wall, and he retreated to his perch near his drink but didn't touch it.

"No, I'm not. I've been doing some research since I saw you earlier—and some thinking. Your story just doesn't wash."

If he was deeply wounded, Crenshaw concealed it well. He looked like a man who had been inconvenienced, but only mildly, as if his pen had run out of ink. "And what story is that, Mr. Goodey?"

"You've got to have another motive than grandfatherly love," I said bluntly.

"Must I?"

"Yes," I said. "I'm sure you're a clever businessman, but you were probably a lousy grandfather. And when it comes to playing the grief-stricken old man, you're way out of your field. I'm sure you'd like to know who killed Katie, but that's not what you've hired me to do. You want me to prove that somebody at The Institute did it. There's a big difference."

Crenshaw seemed to ignore what I'd just said. "Mr. Goodey," he said calmly, "do you make a habit of insulting your clients?"

"Sometimes I have to," I said, "when they lie to me or withhold useful information."

"Perhaps it would be better if you just returned my retainer and left this hotel room."

"Perhaps it would," I said, "but I can't. I've already spent a big chunk of it."

That gave him something to think about. Crenshaw sucked his cheeks in and eyed me with mild disgust. "Is that your idea of professional integrity? Accepting a client's money, *spending* that money and then calling him a liar in an effort to be relieved of your assignment?"

"I don't want to lose this job," I said. "I *like* this job. I like your money. But I want to go to The Institute tomorrow knowing as much as I can. As much as *you* know, if that's possible."

"Tomorrow? You're going down there that soon?" Crenshaw's face melted slightly. "And you think Fischer will be willing to let you in?"

"Better than that. I've had a personal invitation from the great man himself."

"I am reluctantly impressed, Mr. Goodey—if what you say is true."

"It is."

He thought for a moment. "And what if I tell you no more than I already have? What will you do then?"

"I'll still go. But if I fail, we'll both know that at least part of the reason was that you held out on me. And I won't be as cut up about it as I might be."

"But I don't understand how letting you in on my personal business could help you find Katharine's killer. Surely, the facts of her death are the same."

"Perhaps," I said, "but it wasn't just your business, was it? Katie *was* involved," I added, going way beyond my knowledge. I looked at my watch. "Come on, Mr. Crenshaw. I want to get to bed. Either tell me or don't."

"Last November," Crenshaw began smoothly, as if none of all that had been said, "Katharine came down to Los

Angeles to see me. She came alone, and I have to admit that she looked good, better than she had in a couple of years. I'd almost forgotten how pretty, how vibrant she could be. Katharine claimed that she was happier than she'd been in her life and completely free of her dependence on barbiturates."

"Did you believe her?"

"I wanted to," Crenshaw said. "I wouldn't have challenged her anyway. I wanted it to be a happy visit."

"And was it?"

He gave me a dry look. "Not entirely. It was not purely a personal visit. Katharine asked me to turn over to her the three million dollar trust fund left to her by my late wife. As executor of the trust, I had the power to decide whether Katharine, once she'd turned twenty-one, should receive the principal amount of the trust or just the interest on the money. I also had the power to give Katharine her inheritance before her twenty-first birthday, *if* I considered it appropriate."

"That's some power," I said. "And did you consider it appropriate?"

"I did not."

"How did Katie take that?"

"Very badly," Crenshaw said. "She became emotional, almost hysterical."

"So much for the therapeutic benefits of The Institute," I said. "Did she say why she wanted the money?"

"She didn't have to. I'm certain that Fischer and the others at The Institute were working on Katharine to get her money."

"If they were," I said, "they were being pretty successful. What did she do then?"

Crenshaw said, almost sadly: "Katharine threatened to go to the newspapers, to tell the world that I was holding back her money because I hated The Institute. The last thing I wanted was that kind of publicity. Besides, I didn't want to alienate Katharine. I loved my granddaughter, Mr. Goodey. She was the last living member of my family. I had hopes that The Institute would prove to be only a passing phase in her life. That she would—"

"Come back to you?"

Crenshaw looked embarrassed to express such sentiment. "Yes."

"So what did you do?"

"I succeeded in calming Katharine down, and we had quite a reasonable talk. We came to a compromise under which I agreed to her claiming the entire amount of the trust when she was twenty-three years old. That way, she would be able to give The Institute a large lump sum of money, and I could be more certain that she knew what she was doing. In the meantime—once she was twenty-one—she could start collecting a very nice sum in annual interest. Do you know what the annual interest is on three million dollars, Mr. Goodey?

"I dream about it all the time," I said. "That's very nice footwork, Mr. Crenshaw. And now that Katharine is dead, what happens to all that money, under the terms of the trust?"

"It reverts to me. Under the terms of the trust, I was the principal heir. Except for a modest income left to her mother, I was to get the money from the trust."

"So you're home free," I said. "What's the problem?"

"The problem," said Crenshaw meaningfully, "is that as part of our agreement, the money in trust became part of

Katharine's estate. And at the same time, she made a new will leaving everything to Hugo Fischer for the benefit of The Institute. I made Katharine promise not to tell anyone of our arrangement or the new will, but less than a month later she was dead."

"You think she told someone."

"I know that someone at The Institute killed Katharine for the money," Crenshaw said positively.

"That is yet to be proved," I said. "However, it would seem that, under her will, Katie's money is now Fischer's money."

"Technically, that would be true," Crenshaw said, "if Katharine's new will should come to light."

"But it hasn't yet?"

"No," Crenshaw said. "It hasn't. And it won't—if I can prevent it—until you find out who killed my granddaughter."

"I suppose you know," I said, "what you're fooling with. To a jury, it could look an awful lot like fraud, deception, malfeasance as executor of Katie's trust fund, and a lot of other nasty things that could add up to a long stretch in jail."

"I'm fully aware of that, Mr. Goodey," he said. "And the longer I have to keep the will a secret, the greater the danger becomes. So far, Fischer has been cunning enough not to press too hard, but my position could become untenable within a very short time. That is why you must do the job I hired you to do. Once Katharine's killer is discovered, I can use that information to delay things further. You are aware that under law the perpetrator of a crime cannot be allowed to profit from that crime?"

"I've heard something to that effect."

"That is what I am counting on. Once Katharine's

murderer is discovered, the will shall be made public, and I'll be quite content to take my chances in the courts of law. With the responsibility for Katharine's death laid at Fischer's door, her new will has to be ruled invalid. The money from the trust will revert to me and be put to its proper use."

This was a lot for me to take in, so I just sat there and enjoyed his profile for a while. Crenshaw didn't seem to mind. "Mr. Crenshaw," I said at last, "I can't help thinking that you are taking some terrific risks with your personal liberty. To me, three million dollars is a lot of money, and I can understand your reluctance to see it go to Fischer, but wouldn't it be simpler just to let Fischer have the money as Katie intended him to?"

Crenshaw didn't answer for a few seconds, but something seemed to be happening behind his cool facade. For the first time, he looked weary. "Yes, it would, Mr. Goodey," he said. "But the money isn't available right at this moment to give to Fischer."

That stopped me. "And just where is Katie's three million dollars, Mr. Crenshaw?" I asked when I recovered the power of speech.

"Safely invested," Crenshaw said a bit sharply, apparently not crazy about my tone of voice. "Don't think me a thief, Mr. Goodey. As trustee, I have every right to invest Katharine's trust in any manner I choose."

"But..." He was leaving something unsaid.

"I have used Katharine's inheritance to protect some of my own investments," he said. "Not bad investments, but situations which will require a bit of time to come to fruition. At this time..."

"What would happen at this time if Fischer demanded Katharine's money? Could it be realized?"

"Yes," said Crenshaw bleakly, "every cent. But to pull

that three million dollars out at this time would ruin me completely. My investments would be worthless, and I would be all but a pauper."

"How long do you need to hold on to Katharine's money?"

"At least another three months. By then the business situation will have improved enough so that I could withdraw the money from the trust."

"You hope."

"It must!" Some of the snap came back into Crenshaw's delivery. "Have you ever been poor, Mr. Goodey?"

"I've never been anything else."

"Well, I have," he said firmly, "and I'm never going to be poor again. I'd rather be dead. I will be before too much longer, anyway, but I must have my own fortune and Katherine's to..."

"To what, Mr. Crenshaw?" I said. "Don't be shy. I already know enough to deliver you to both the police and the bankruptcy court. What have you got to lose?"

"Nothing," he said, "but it's none of your business."

"That's what you told me about what you've just told me," I said. "Go the whole route, Mr. Crenshaw. Enlighten me. I won't laugh."

I could see from his expression that the possibility had never occurred to him. "You're right, Mr. Goodey," he said. "I may as well tell you the whole story. It doesn't matter what you think."

I nodded encouragingly.

He began: "Mr. Goodey, I wasn't being dramatic when I said that I will not live long. My doctors are not encouraging, to put it mildly. And when I die it will mean the end of my family. I won't pretend to you that it has been an exalted family thus far. My father was a bartender. But I had hoped that Bud—my son—with the advantages that I was able to give him and his mother's inheritance, would go on to do some really good things with his life. But Bud didn't come back from Korea.

"Then, to be frank, I'd hoped that his child would be a boy—Frederick Melhuish Crenshaw III." He smiled ruefully. "But that didn't work out as I'd planned, either. I ended up pinning all my hopes on Katharine, even if she didn't bear the family name. And you know, Mr. Goodey, what that has come to."

Crenshaw plunged: "It may seem pointless vanity to you, but I want my name to live on after I am dead. It must. That is why I must continue to use Katharine's money to safeguard my own. I then intend to use every cent at my command to endow a foundation—the Frederick Melhuish Crenshaw Jr. Foundation—to ensure that poor but promising boys, as I once was, Mr. Goodey, will have a chance at a good education whether or not they are athletes, as I had the good fortune to be.

"Even if my name survives only in this way, it will survive. I will not stand by and see myself ruined and my son's inheritance go to a fraud like Hugo Fischer, simply for him to use for further self-aggrandizement."

I could have said that it was probably a photo finish between him and Fischer in the self-aggrandizement stakes, but I didn't. I just stood up and said: "Thank you for being so honest with me, Mr. Crenshaw." And I went home.

Back in my apartment, I stacked the two reports under half a bottle of villainous Sonoma Valley Grenache rosé, turned off the lights and retreated to my long, narrow bedroom with the spectacular view. I got into bed and lay there watching cars cross the Richmond-San Rafael Bridge, thinking about Crenshaw's dilemma. In the alley below a convention of Chinatown's cat population was in good voice. The last thing I heard was either a strangled cry for help or the beginning of a lasting friendship.

5

I woke up the next morning, which, in my business, is about as much as you can expect. For a moment I just lay there wondering how to best kill the day and avoid my creditors. Or vice versa. Then I remembered that I'd promised to do a little job for Fred Crenshaw. And that I had some of his money left in my pocket. There's nothing like money up front to inspire my sense of responsibility, so I got out of bed. After a ritual cup of coffee and a peek out of the window—weather fair but with a slight overcast that would burn off—I threw some clothes in my old suitcase. I hadn't thought to ask Rachel what they wore at The Institute. If it turned out to be flowing djellabahs and toe-thong sandals, I was going to stick out like a nun in Las Vegas. I didn't pack my tux.

There are three ways to drive to Monterey from San Francisco. My favorite is little Highway 1 hugging the coastline with its dumpy beach towns, smog-belching power plants and second-rate redwood forests. I didn't try to break any speed records. The Morris had developed something in the sweetbreads which sounded pretty terminal, and I dared not push it too hard.

I got to Monterey just before noon and had to look for the sheriff's new office. The old one had been razed, and just about where the desk sergeant used to lean, a teenager was selling chilidogs to the unwary. A leathery old Mexican confused me with elaborate directions, but eventually I stowed the Morris in a parking slot for "Monterey County Sheriff's Office Personnel only" and walked into the modernistic building, which only slightly resembled a pop-up toaster.

Just for the fun of it, I told the young deputy behind the desk that I wanted to see Sheriff Dominguez. Assuming that I was drunk, he signaled for a couple of weightlifters to help me out to the sidewalk. He called them off when I flashed my private operative's license. I don't think he was all that impressed; maybe he just didn't want them to get their hands dirty.

"I wouldn't want to pry into your business, Mr. Good-ey," the deputy said, "but you couldn't see Sheriff Dominguez even if you had a note from God. I've been on this force three and a half years, and I've seen him only twice—once by accident."

"It's not really a state secret," I said. "I'm looking into the death of the Pierce girl down at Las Palomas last December."

"Another one," he said, his face going a bit slack.

"Yep," I said, trying not to sound too cheerful. "But..."

"Not another word." He raised an ink-stained hand. "My contract says I don't have to talk about Katie Pierce or The Institute. On Saturday I don't have to talk at all. You just wait one minute, and I'll get you someone who loves to talk about The Institute." He picked up the receiver on the desk and dialed two digits. "Lieutenant?" he said, "I've got another one out here asking about Katie Pierce. No, not Brazewell's bunch. Not the old man, either. It's a private cop from San Francisco name of—" He took another look at my credentials. "—Goodey. Jonah W. Goodey. Okay. Sure."

"You're in luck," the deputy said after he hung up. "Our expert on The Institute has a few minutes to spare." He gestured toward an opaque door marked Investigations. "Just wander through there and ask for Lieutenant Grenby."

It wasn't too hard to find a door that had "Lt. Michael Grenby, Assistant Director of Investigations," on it. It didn't say knock, so I didn't.

The face that looked up at me over a crowded desk was young, nearly as young as that of the deputy outside, but a lot more intelligent. It was the face of a star on the D.A.'s staff or a first-term congressman. It was the kind of face that makes you wonder how it ever got on a cop. His hair was dark and curly and just slightly longer than was absolutely necessary. Behind aviator-style spectacles, his eyes were friendly without being effusive.

"Mr. Goodey," he said. "Won't you have a chair?"

I did, and we sat facing each other in perfect silence for a few seconds. It was very restful.

"Would I be wrong in assuming that Mr. Crenshaw sent you down here?" he asked.

"Sent is a bit strong," I said. "Crenshaw hired me to find out how his granddaughter died, and I'm on my way down to Las Palomas to do that."

"Just like that?"

"Well, maybe not just like that, Lieutenant," I said. "But can you think of a better place than Las Palomas to find out just how Katie Pierce came to die last December?"

"I know how Katie Pierce died," he said, with slight impatience and more than slight weariness. "I spent weeks of my life on that job. The county paid me to do it. What do you think you can do down at Las Palomas except waste more of Crenshaw's money?"

"I don't know," I admitted, "but I'm not going to sting him for nearly as much as Brazewell did. I might just find something out. Are you one-hundred percent positive that it was an accident or suicide?"

It was his turn to make an admission. "No, I'm not that sure of anything. But I wasn't able to turn up anything that indicated that it wasn't, either. You've seen my report?"

I hesitated, not wanting to give anything away. But he added quickly: "Don't worry, Mr. Goodey. I know you've got it, and I know who gave it to you. The man lost his only grandchild, and I'm not the stuffy sort who objects to a little bribery and violation of confidential documents if it will finally convince Crenshaw that nobody's hiding anything about Katie's death. God knows I'm not."

Grenby continued: "Aside from anything else, I don't like open coroner's reports. They're untidy and they make me nervous. If you can settle the matter to Crenshaw's satisfaction, I'm on your side all the way. I don't dare to have a nightmare these days for fear of finding Crenshaw in it."

"He seems a bit persistent," I agreed.

"And Bluebeard was a bit of a ladies' man," Grenby said. "Does Hugo—does Fischer know you're coming down to The Institute?"

"Yes. He kindly allowed one of his minions, Dr. James Carey, to invite me last night." I paused and then added: "So you won't have to tell him."

He didn't like that. He was still deciding just how much

he didn't like it when I stood up and politely thanked him for his time.

Grenby ignored my gratitude. When he spoke he was trying to keep his tone professional and detached. "I think you're wasting your time, Mr. Goodey, but there's no way that I can stop you from going down to The Institute. Nor would I want to. But I would suggest that you watch your step while you're in Monterey County. This is not San Francisco."

I thanked Grenby for the advice, not to mention the geography lesson, and carried on down the coast toward Las Palomas. Just below Carmel, my stomach began threatening industrial action, so I pulled off the highway into the parking lot of Nepenthe, a redwood and plate-glass fantasy hanging over the sea. The day had grown even finer, so I sat outside with the big, open-pit fireplace at my back, alternately admiring the incredible sea views and the waitress's bobbling breasts.

Crenshaw was paying, so I went the whole hog and ordered the ambrosia burger, a basket of French fries and a pitcher of beer. The change left out of ten bucks wasn't worth worrying about, so I gave it to the waitress. She wasn't overwhelmed.

"Have you heard of a place called The Institute?" I asked her as she cleared the table.

"It's that bunch of nuts down in Las Palomas, isn't it?" she said, not too diplomatically. "Some of them come here once in a while. They don't seem to be short of money." I said I thought we were talking about the same place and asked if she'd ever been there.

"No," she said. "There are enough freaks and weirdos in Big Sur without going to look for more. You going down there?"

"Yes," I said. "I understand they've got some kind of a new lifestyle. I want to find out what it's all about."

"You a journalist?" she demanded, but another customer caught her eye with an urgent semaphore before I could answer.

Once I was on the highway again, the sunshine, the blue sky and the broad vista of surf crashing against the rocky shore exercised a hypnotic effect, and I was nearly into Lucia before I realized that I'd passed right by The Institute. Turning around, I was a bit more alert and eventually spotted a discreet wooden sign reading "The Institute" resting in some shrubbery beside an inconspicuous dirt road on the seaward side of the highway. An equally circumspect notice said: "Private Property—Trespassers Will Be Prosecuted."

Making a mental note of that fact, I turned the Morris down the dirt road, which quickly became a green tunnel of foliage with only glancing penetration of sunlight. It seemed like clear sailing until I'd turned the second curve and found a railroad-type barrier across the road. It was manned by two young blacks wearing gray coveralls of the sort mechanics wear. I stopped the car, and one of them walked over with an official look on his face.

"Excuse me, sir," he said. "May I ask your business at The Institute?"

I told him I was an invited guest and gave him my name. He consulted his clipboard until he recognized one of the names on it. "Welcome to The Institute, Mr. Goodey," he said. "May I see your identification?"

Not sure whether I wanted to alert the lower orders, I showed him my California driver's license. The picture on it isn't a very good likeness; I'm really handsomer and have much more hair. But he nodded, said "Thank you," and gestured to his associate to lift the barrier.

I drove on. I couldn't help admiring The Institute's security arrangements, but then I've always been a sucker for good security. The road ahead continued to twist gently downhill, passing through stands of silver pine and eucalyptus until, quite suddenly, it opened onto a broad vista of unnaturally green grass—acres of it—running down to a mansion like a baroque wedding cake. I couldn't place the period, but it was someplace between mock-Byzantine and Gay Nineties Gothic. I didn't have much time to study the architecture before my attention was grabbed by the spectacle in front of the mansion.

There on the grass was something resembling a production of *A Midsummer Night's Dream* as done by a tank-building collective in Omsk. Almost everyone was wearing coveralls, but the colors ranged from palest pastel shades to dark greens, blues and browns, plus a heavy sprinkling of drab gray.

These pixies seemed to be performing some sort of ritual involving a lot of flowers and heavy breathing. At first I couldn't figure it out, but then I remembered that Rachel had said something about a wedding. Then I spotted the bride and groom in identical pink coveralls, leis of white flowers around their necks and wreaths on their heads, which were at that moment bowed in front of a bearded gentleman all decked out like the high priest of camp. I parked the car and joined the fringe of the throng.

Even from where I stood, there was a remarkable contrast between the bowed heads of the bridal couple. His bore the scars and wrinkles of over sixty years of hard times. What little hair he had was elaborately pushed around to cover the naked bits of a bullet dome. The bride, on the other hand, hadn't weathered more than about twenty summers and had the profile of a fallen angel. Her large dark eyes were lowered in stagey solemnity.

As I was admiring this misalliance, the bearded one must have said the magic words because the mob went crazy. The air was full of confetti, balloons and flowers, and most of the celebrants converged on the blissful pair. But not Rachel Schute, who was coming at me from the crowd towing a none-too-eager Dr. James Carey behind her.

"Joe," Rachel called, "I'm glad you didn't miss the wedding. Wasn't it beautiful?"

I grunted something noncommittal.

"Come on," she said. "I want you to meet Hugo." She turned, and I followed her gaze to a flower-overwhelmed bower, where the newlyweds were receiving the blessings of a figure in virginal-white coveralls. Hugo Fischer, I presumed. He was a thick man, blocky rather than fat, and his close-cropped, fur-like hair running nearly down to his eyebrows gave him a slightly animal look. At that moment, he was deep in conversation with the bride and groom, and his heavy features held an expression of total benevolence. He was the patriarchal figure deep in the bosom of his family. The bridegroom was well over ten years his senior, but basked in Fischer's smile like a seal pup on a sunny rock.

Fischer wound up his benediction with a showy kiss on the bride's ivory brow. Then he turned in our direction and was suddenly transformed. The left side of his face, hidden from me until then, was scarred with a livid, purple-red birthmark, which spread from his throat to his eyebrow like a flaming growth.

The effect was startling. The birthmark turned Fischer into a flawed idol, half-benign, half-malevolent. On the disfigured side of his face, his mouth seemed to turn down in a slight but perpetual scowl, and the eye wreathed in the dying tentacles of the birthmark had a saturnine cast.

Rachel was urging me toward Fischer when a girl in pale green coveralls approached him from the side and said something. Fischer inclined the disfigured side of his face toward her, and as he listened, his expression changed radically. The benevolent father was superseded by an outraged and angry god.

Straightening up, Fischer filled his bull-like chest and bellowed: "Form the circle!"

The effect on the crowd on the grass was instantaneous. One moment they were an aimless, happy rabble scattered over the lawn like sheep, talking, laughing, taking food and drink from long trestle tables. Then they were like so many iron filings obeying the dictates of a magnetic force. As if operating with one consciousness, all of the mob in coveralls spread swiftly but deliberately across the lawn, joining hands as they moved, until they were formed into a circle some fifty yards across with Fischer at twelve o'clock, standing with his back to the mansion's oak double doors.

Rachel and I and a number of other plainclothes visitors were left on the periphery of the circle. Rachel didn't seem particularly surprised by this development, but my mouth was hanging open. The faces of the residents that I could see seemed to go blank yet expectant at the same time. I noticed that Carey had left Rachel's side and had slipped into the circle at Fischer's left hand.

Fischer checked to see that the circle was complete and began to raise his hand in signal to someone off to one side. Then, at Fischer's right hand, another figure in white, a slim, sallow-faced woman in her mid-forties with something haggard and haunted in her features, caught Fischer's wrist lightly. She said something to him that I was too far away to hear. But her expression was pleading.

Fischer threw off her hand easily and finished the signal. "Yes!" he said in a booming voice. "Especially today."

The ceremonial circle broke slightly at one point, and an escort of twelve fair-sized men in two gray columns marched into the circle led by a thin, hawk-like man in black. Between their ranks were a boy and girl not in coveralls. The circle closed like water behind them, and the phalanx pivoted smartly and stopped in front of Hugo Fischer.

"For God's sake, Rachel," I said. "What's going on? Who are these people? I don't have a program."

"*Shhh*," she shushed me. Her eyes were riveted on Fischer.

"You'd better tell me," I warned her, "or I'll do something human, like start laughing. Who's the woman in white, for a start?"

"Lenore Fischer," she whispered, just to shut me up. "Hugo's wife."

The bodyguard in gray peeled away with military precision leaving the character in black and the young couple in the middle of the circle. Their attitudes were a study in contrast. The couple stood with eyes downcast, as if caught in an act of original sin. The man in black stood ramrod straight, his zealot's eyes locked on Fischer's impassive face. He was about thirty-five, and had a face like a hammer.

"Identify," I whispered, jabbing Rachel in the ribs.

"Don Moffitt," she said with resignation. "Vice President of the Institute."

At that moment, Moffitt jabbed his chin at the sky and said in a voice loud enough to be heard in Big Sur: "As you can see, Hugo, two of our lost sheep have returned."

"What do they want?" Fischer asked, in a voice edged with malignant bonhomie. He was playing to the back rows and looked to be all set for a good time.

"They say," Moffitt intoned, "that they want back in. They want to rejoin our community."

"The hell they do!" pronounced Fischer, sticking his lower lip out like Mussolini.

"What did they do?" I asked Rachel.

"They left The Institute without permission—together," Rachel said, without taking her eyes from the spectacle. "Two weeks ago."

"That *was* naughty," I said, but Rachel wasn't listening.

"Why?" asked Fischer like a clap of thunder. "What can they want here? Perhaps they can tell me. What do you want of me? What do you want of your former brothers and sisters? Speak!"

The boy, tall, gaunt and Byronic with thick, curly black hair covering his ears, raised his dark-browed eyes toward Fischer in near defiance. But he couldn't hold it, and let his eyes fall to the toes of his dusty cowboy boots. The girl, slight and fair and dressed gypsy style, didn't raise her face at all. Her hair hung lank and knotted.

"Speak to Hugo," Moffitt demanded. "He asked you a question."

The boy's lips moved hesitantly, but not much came out.

"Speak up!" barked Moffitt, and someone from the circle shouted:

"We can't hear you, Lennie."

The boy tried again, the strain showing on his face, and his voice came out broken and unmodulated as from a faulty radio. "We want to come back," he said, "because we need The Institute." He dropped his head again.

"But we don't need you!" bawled Moffitt, and he was echoed by growls from around the circle.

"Throw 'em out on the highway," called Dr. James Carey, in a tone remarkably like Fischer's.

"Give 'em a dollar and put them on the road," cried the bridegroom. His voice was raspy, his face contorted with suddenly summoned indignation. "We don't need these bums."

"Who the hell is the old geezer?" I whispered to Rachel.

"Pops Martin," she said shortly. "A founding member of The Institute."

Fischer swiveled his large head angrily in our direction, and Rachel went a deep pink. Then he turned his attention back to the more grievous sinners.

After looking at the couple for a long moment, he asked almost casually: "What do you think, Mark?"

A half dozen places to his left, a swarthy guy in his mid-twenties, tall but soft looking, as if he hadn't yet lost all of his baby fat, preened himself for a moment and then replied in an adenoidal voice: "I can't help wondering, Hugo, just how much they want back in."

That must have been the right thing to say, for immediately other voices around the circle took up the cry.

"Yeah, how much?"

"Tell us!"

"Beg, you motherfuckers!"

"Yes, beg! Beg!" The mob took up this popular cry all around the circle.

I nudged Rachel again, but she ignored me.

"Who's the big baby doing the rabblerousing?" I demanded, but Rachel didn't know I was there.

"His name is Mark Kinsey," said a woman's soft voice behind us. I turned around to find a fellow spectator, a middle-aged suburban matron in a very subtle blue rinse, looking at me with some irritation. "He's The Institute's press officer," she added, "and we'd all appreciate it if you'd shut up."

I thanked her none too warmly for the information and considered asking her who she thought she was, but decided against it. When I turned back to the spectacle, the crowd was still demanding that Lennie and his girlfriend prove just how sincerely they wanted to be back in the loving bosom of The Institute. Those two weren't saying anything, just studying the grass in front of their feet as if one of them had dropped a dime.

At that moment, Hugo Fischer raised a pair of substantial arms, and the clamor died down until the silence was so complete that I could detect that someone behind me had a mild case of asthma.

"Barbara," said Fischer in a gentle tone that didn't convince me one hundred percent, "look at me."

Nothing much happened, and the silence piled up like snow on a frail branch. Something had to break. It turned out to be the girl. Slowly, painfully, she raised her dirty, tear-stained face until she was looking at Hugo Fischer. Her vague eyes blinked as if she were looking into the sun.

"That's better," said Fischer benignly. "You look, Barbara, as if you've had a hard couple of weeks."

The girl said nothing. Her face was blank with exhaustion. She swayed slightly, and the boy at her side reached automatically toward her. Waves of convulsion seemed to rock her body; she opened her mouth wider than I would have thought possible and cried: "Hugo! Please let us back in! I—please!" She put her hands to her face and slipped to her knees. Instantly, Lennie was kneeling beside her and pulling her matted head to his chest, but everybody else froze. With effort, I pulled my eyes from Barbara and Lennie to see how Fischer was taking it.

I'm not learned enough to describe the expression on Fischer's face at that moment. It wasn't triumph, nothing as petty as that. If anything, it was a sort of heroic, grieved satisfaction such as God might have worn if Adam and Eve had applied for readmission to the Garden of Eden.

I found it hard to take, and was just about to find something else for my eyes to do when Fischer clapped his hands and signaled to Moffitt. "Take them away," he said in a magisterial voice and turned away. As if it had been the creation of a magic spell, the circle was gone. The coveralled members of The Institute were a celebrating throng again, and Pops Martin and his blushing bride were the focus of attention. The cordon in gray disappeared with its prisoners.

At my side, Rachel stood very still in a trance. I couldn't think of much to say myself, so I just stood there and marveled quietly.

Then Rachel seemed to shake the spell and said: "Now, we'll find Hugo, and I'll introduce you to—" We both looked in the direction where Fischer had been, but he'd vanished. She was looking around when a voice said:

"Rachel, it's lovely to see you again." It was the woman who had politely told me to shut my face.

Rachel, who seemed glad to have something to do, said: "Hello, Eloise. Did you know?"

Eloise shook her head. "No. So far as I knew, they were nowhere near here. It was a great shock to me when they suddenly appeared like that."

"I don't like to be rude, Eloise," I said, "but my name is Joe Goodey, and I haven't a clue what you're talking about."

Rachel did the honorable thing and introduced us. She

said that Eloise was Mrs. Barker, a local supporter of The Institute.

"I'm happy to meet you, Mr. Goodey," Eloise said, "and I want to apologize to you for being so rude earlier. But we take ceremonies very seriously at The Institute. If you'll excuse me, I've got to go see someone." She smiled opaquely and disappeared into the crowd.

"Who," I asked Rachel, "was that?"

"That," said Rachel, "was Barbara's mother."

"Barbara?" I said blankly, but then the realization hit me. "Not—"

"Yes," she said, "that Barbara."

Rachel got a slightly smug, pedagogic look on her face and said: "It's not really as inexplicable as you might think, Joe. Barbara is a girl with very serious emotional problems. She's been at The Institute for only three months, and she was making very good progress until recently when she and Lennie got too—too attracted to each other. He's an ex-drug addict who came to The Institute from New Jersey."

"So?" I said.

"So, Hugo banned Barbara and Lennie from seeing each other—for their own good. Two weeks ago they ran off together. And today they came back."

"I can handle all that pretty well," I said. "But what bothers me is that you all—even the girl's mother—could just stand here and watch Fischer and his mad dogs play with that girl as if she were a bundle of rags."

There was a pitying look in Rachel's eyes when she said: "Joe, you just don't understand. Hugo is trying to save those children's lives. You've got an awful lot to learn about The Institute."

"I'll say," I said.

6

BEFORE I COULD SAY ANYTHING MORE, AN ANEMIC BOY in pale blue coveralls was tugging on Rachel's sleeve.

"Rachel," he said, "Hugo is waiting to see you in his office. And your visitor."

So my arrival hadn't gone unnoticed at the highest levels. Perhaps the good Dr. Carey had whispered something in Hugo Fischer's sizeable ear.

"Thank you, Glynn," Rachel said, and she and I started walking up the drive toward the vast oak doors, which were now open. The celebrating residents and their guests were drifting freely between the lawn and the mansion. A band was playing in a large marquee at one side of the big house, and merriment was unrestrained. We pushed our way through the mob into the foyer of the mansion. It was a splendid house; someone had spent a fortune on the marble floor alone, but there was something odd and institutional about the atmosphere. I kept expecting an announcement to come blasting out of a loud-speaker.

I climbed the immaculate marble staircase at Rachel's

side. "How do I address this Fischer character?" I asked. "Your Lordship, or will a simple Sir do?"

"Everybody at The Institute," said Rachel without a glimmer of a smile, "calls him Hugo. You're no exception."

On the first floor, we turned down a wide, cream colored hall. The carpets were Oriental and looked expensive. Rachel stopped outside an unmarked door from behind which I heard a low murmur of voices. She knocked softly, and the voices died.

"Come in," called a familiar voice, a bit impatiently. When I pushed the door open, Fischer was sitting facing the door behind about a quarter acre of executive-style desk, flanked by Carey and the hard man in black, Don Moffitt. Pops Martin, a couple of pink petals still lodged in his thin locks, sat on an easy chair in front of a bay window, one leg cocked over the opposite bony knee. Mark Kinsey was perched on the opposite window sill, practicing an institutional rock and looking insecure. The walls of the office were crowded with framed 9-by-12 inch signed photographs of that same quartet and others who I assumed were big shots of The Institute. It looked like a parody of a third-rate movie producer's office.

Rachel followed me into the room and shut the door. For lack of anything else to do, I stopped in front of Fischer and waited for him to say something. He didn't disappoint me.

"What the hell do you want here, Goodwin?" he demanded.

A fair question that deserved an honest answer.

"The name is Goodey, Mr. Fischer, G-double-o-d-e-y, Joe Goodey," I said. "And I've come here to find out which of you murdered Katharine Pierce."

Fischer soaked it up without showing much response at

all, but his honchos each reacted in a typical way. Carey let his jaw drop at my rudeness and started thinking about getting angry; Moffitt balled his fists ready for action; Kinsey rocked back a bit abruptly, hit his head against the windowpane and looked embarrassed. Only old Pops Martin did anything very active. He uncoiled himself from the chair faster than I'd have thought possible and came toward me like a small dog on a short leash. Planting both gnarled hands on the top of Fischer's desk, he got a fierce expression on his old mug and snarled: "Watch your lip, shamus—or you'll find yourself waking up in the gutter with your head on a dead cat."

The word shamus went out of style in about 1938 and Martin couldn't have whipped his weight in macaroons, but I had to give him points for originality. I'd have to think about that one. He was about to get off something even more horrific when Fischer yanked gently on his leash.

"Easy, Pops," he said. "Don't forget that this is your wedding day. I'm sure our visitor isn't being deliberately provocative." Pops retired to his chair with a nonchalant slouch, but his eyes served notice that I was on probation.

Fischer turned back to me and then had to lower his line of sight because I'd sat down on a very nice chair nobody seemed to be using. He didn't much like the idea, but he'd get used to it. Rachel had retired to a couch out of the line of fire, and Carey was sending her obscure signals with his eyebrows. She was too busy eyeing Fischer with nervous apprehension to notice.

"You take a radical line of approach, boy," Fischer said. "It may have been a success with the San Francisco Police Department," he added, not without irony, "but it won't get you far in my house. What makes you think I won't have my good friends here pitch you right back on Highway One?"

"Because I've got a feeling that you'd like this mess cleared up once and for all if only to get Crenshaw off your back."

"Mr. Crenshaw," Fischer said, "is a very unhappy man. When he was here, we did everything we could to convince him that Katie's death was an accident, a tragic accident, but nothing more. No one here could have or would have killed Katie. There is no mess here to clear up, Mr. Goodey."

"That's your story," I said, "but I imagine that you can understand why Crenshaw feels a bit differently. And why he hired me. Sure, you can throw me out of here, but it won't satisfy Crenshaw a bit. He's got the idea that I can find out exactly how she died. He may be mistaken, but I'm the best bet you've got right now. That is, unless you'd like to be a perpetual target for Crenshaw's paranoia."

Fischer thought that over for a moment. He reached up and scratched his skull through his close-cropped hair. "Mr. Goodey," he said at last, "you may have something. Frankly, I'm tired of holding open house for nosey private detectives. We've got nothing to hide here, but I get kind of tired of answering the same stupid questions. How long do you think it'll take you to satisfy yourself and Mr. Crenshaw?"

"I couldn't say," I answered. "With luck, you may not have to feed me tonight. Or I could stay around to be your oldest living guest."

"Just do your best," Fischer said, a bit wearily. "Mark, please find Mr. Goodey some place to sleep."

Kinsey leapt off his window sill, and I got the uneasy feeling that we'd both been dismissed. I wasn't quite ready yet.

"I'm assuming, Mr. Fischer," I said from my comfortable

chair, "that I'm going to be given a certain amount of coop-eration in my investigations."

Fischer looked back toward me as if I were an ashtray that he distinctly remembered ordering to be emptied. "Mr. Goodey," he said, "to you The Institute is an open book. You have only to ask. If anyone gives you any problems, I will solve them for you." He quickly glanced to see if his minions had taken this in. "Now," he said emphatically, "I will be very happy to see you later."

Kinsey was already at the door, dancing with eagerness to carry out his orders, so I got up and prepared to follow him.

"One little thing, Mr. Goodey," Fischer said to my back. I turned around. "You wouldn't happen to be carrying some sort of firearm on your person, would you?"

I admitted as much, my police special being at that moment tucked snugly under my armpit in a shoulder holster.

"We've got a few rules here, Mr. Goodey," he said. "One of which is no firearms of any kind." He held out a large hand. "I'll just keep your weapon here for you until you leave." He was doing me a favor.

I thought for a moment, and then handed it over. I hadn't been planning to shoot anyone anyway. He slid open a desk drawer, and my pistol disappeared. I turned back toward the door. "So long, Rachel," I said. "See you later." But she wasn't paying much attention.

Kinsey set off down the hall at a fairly good pace, and I ambled along behind him, taking in the luxurious surround-ings. When he discovered that somebody was dogging it, he dropped back reluctantly to my side.

"You people do all right for yourselves here," I said, just to make conversation. "This place must have cost a fortune."

"The mansion was given to us," he said, rather sniffily. "Besides, it's not the surroundings that count."

"All the same," I said, "it probably beats sleeping rough. How many acres has the place got?"

"Something over four hundred and fifty," he said, "including the land on the other side of the highway. With nearly a half mile of beachfront." He said it with a quiet pride.

"Tell me," I asked him, "how'd you come to join a place like this? You weren't a secret glue sniffer, were you?"

"Not exactly," Kinsey said, not too unfriendly. "A couple of years ago, the Institute jazz band—you heard them playing in the marquee on the lawn—made a record album. I was doing public relations for the record company, and I came up here from L.A. to do research for the liner notes. I met Hugo, took a look at what he had going here, and discovered that my life was shit, my work was shit and my future was shit."

"That sounds pretty shitty," I said.

"It was. So I went back to Los Angeles, finished the album notes, quit my job, piled everything I owned into my car and drove back up here. I've been here ever since."

"And happy with it?" I asked.

"Not entirely," he said honestly, "but it beats being a whore for a record company."

Kinsey led me down a dark flight of stairs into what must have been a household work area in the old days. We paraded along a deserted hallway until we came to a small room with "Housing Office" painted on the wall beside an open Dutch door. Inside the closet-like room, an olive-skinned guy in his mid-twenties was hunched over a ledger, biting his lower lip. He looked up as we approached. He had a biggish nose, a hard mouth and streetwise eyes. His hair was chopped into something spikey, and he looked as though he could handle himself. He wore his dark blue coveralls with natural authority.

"Jack," said Mark Kinsey, "this is Joe Goodey. He's a guest of The Institute. Find him a bed to sleep in, will you?" He turned to me: "This is Jack Gillette. He'll take care of you."

Gillette looked down at his ledger book. "I'll just put you in the Starlight Suite, if that's okay with you."

"Sounds fine."

He looked back up at Kinsey. "Thanks, Mark. I'll take care of him and bring him along to the front desk later, okay?"

"That's fine," said Kinsey. "See you later," he added to me and disappeared down the hall.

"Let's go," said Gillette, taking a big ring of keys from a nail on the wall.

As we walked up the back stairs, Gillette asked: "You got a suitcase?"

"In my car," I said.

"Give me your keys," he said, "and I'll have somebody bring it up to your room."

"I can do it myself," I said. "I don't need looking after."

"No sweat. If there's one thing we've got around here, it's manpower."

"All right, then," I said, giving him my keys. "It's the—"

"Beat-up gray Morris convertible, right?"

"Right. What else do you know?"

"You're a private cop from San Francisco who's come down here to try to prove old man Crenshaw's theory that somebody at The Institute gave Katie Pierce the big shove."

"I'd hate to be trying to go undercover," I said. "Does everybody know what I'm up to?"

"They will. The rarest thing here at The Institute is a secret."

"I don't know," I said. "I can think of one."

"You're going to play hell proving it. The sheriff and those superstars from L.A. were all over this place and they didn't find out a thing."

"How do you know?"

"You're here, aren't you? If those Brazewell dudes had proved anything, we'd have had a lot more sheriff's department around here, and not a lone-star operator like you. Frankly, I think Crenshaw is getting a bit desperate."

"Thanks," I said. "Did you talk to the Brazewell people?"

"No," he said, reaching a landing and starting up yet another flight of steps. "But they thought I did. I don't like cops—private or otherwise."

"That's too bad. You going to talk to me?"

"I haven't made up my mind yet." At the next landing, he turned down a faded corridor and stopped in front of a tall, narrow doorway. "Here we are." He shoved the door inward, releasing a musty, off-color smell. He moved into the room, shoved aside some mucus-colored drapes and opened the window wide. "It's not luxury," he said, "but you'll be okay in here."

It sure wasn't luxury. You could have swung a cat in the room, but not a big one, and the sallow wallpaper had been new about the time Teddy Roosevelt fell up San Juan Hill. Some drudge of an under-butler had lived—and probably died—in this room.

"What's that?" I asked, indicating a small, round metal box on the wall above the bed. It was about the size of an old-fashioned car-radio speaker.

"Bitch box," he said "We don't want you to miss anything while you're here, do we?"

"I'll try to live with it." Gillette looked as though he were about to leave, but I asked him: "What did you do before you came here?"

"I hit people on the head and took their money," he said. "That is, if they were small enough and I could get out of jail to do it."

"It's probably the question you hate most," I said, "but how did you find yourself in a sissy outfit like The Institute?"

"I don't mind," he said, thumbing a cigarette up out of a soft pack and offering me one, which I refused. "I can answer that one in my sleep. I was doing a little street-nodding in downtown Los Angeles nearly three years ago, just looking for a nice, soft gutter to lie down in, when I found myself leaning against the plate glass of a storefront The Institute was running down there. A couple of passing cops wanted to do me for molesting the window, when one of the residents came out and made a better offer. Any bed but one in the city slammer looked good to me, so I took it. I figured that once I came down I could rip something off to hock and split."

"Sound thinking," I said.

"It seemed so at the time," Gillette said, exhaling smoke, "but it didn't work out that way. It took a long time, but I really went for the okee dokee and stuck around for the ride."

"Been a pretty good ride, has it?"

"I suppose it depends on what you're used to, but if you look out for flying horseshit, it can be a hell of a lot of fun. Of course, you don't want to get caught up in the insanity too much. That can mess with your oatmeal something terrible."

"I can imagine," I said. "I hope this isn't too personal, but what's the deal with all those gaudy coveralls?"

"Well, as it originally came down from on high about three months ago," he said, thumbing a lapel, "these colorful outfits —to quote Hugo—are a graphic representation of each individual's position on the Rainbow of Life, or some shit like that. Myself, I think he just ran into a fire sale on coveralls that he couldn't resist. Either that, or he just wanted to see what some of these pencil-necks looked like in lime green or magenta. I'm not bothered myself; it saves wear and tear on my own duds."

"You don't seem to take the situation here at The Institute very seriously, Jack," I said.

"Oh, I'm serious enough," he said, "about the big things. I know what I'd be doing if I hadn't fallen in here by accident."

"What's that?"

"Time," he said. "This is the longest I've been out of the slammer since I was eleven years old, and to me that says something. Maybe when I've been here a bit longer, I'll know exactly what. Come on. I'll take you down to the front desk, and Mark will probably pick you up and give you the big picture. I'm not authorized to deal with the big picture."

As we left the room, I asked: "Don't I get a key?"

"There are no keys at The Institute," Gillette said. "Hugo's policy."

"But don't things get stolen?"

"Sure they do," he said. "But not as much as you'd think. We call it redistribution of wealth."

"I'll keep that in mind," I said, but I wasn't crazy about it.

As we walked down the staircase, I asked: "Did you know Katie Pierce?"

"Yeah, I knew her," he said. "I make it my business to know everybody who comes to The Institute."

"Did you know her well?"

"No," he said. "She was cute, but a bit too ring-a-ding for me. Speed does things to your mush that I don't understand or appreciate."

"Who do you think shoved her off the roof?"

"I don't," he said curtly, "and don't come at me with off the wall questions like that. I told you: I think you're wasting your time and Crenshaw's money, but it's okay with me. As long as you don't expect me to get caught up in your insanity. Okay?"

"Okay," I agreed, and we walked the rest of the way downstairs in silence. I didn't know how useful Gillette was going to turn out to be, but he sure as hell wasn't going to do my job for me. When we were on the main floor again, Gillette led me into a big, plush room full of residents and guests chattering and having a good time. Nobody paid any attention to us. One corner of the room had been turned into a kind of office festooned with typed notices, pigeon holes for letters and notes and official looking paperwork in neat stacks.

Behind the desk at that moment was a black dude seven feet tall with a shaved head. He didn't look any too thrilled when Gillette said: "Roscoe, this is Joe Goodey, a guest in the house. Mark said he'd probably pick him up here. Joe, this is Roscoe Matson. He's the house manager. I'll leave you with him."

7

Gillette walked away, leaving me propped against the desk like a beach umbrella. Matson seemed to be bearing up under the responsibility. For quite a while, he doggedly stuck to his knitting and didn't even look up to say howdy.

I passed the time eyeballing what looked a lot like any other exquisitely furnished drawing room full of lounging drug addicts and social misfits. Stuck at various strategic locations on the heavily embossed wallpaper were butcher-paper banners carrying an eclectic variety of quotes from usually reliable sources ranging from Mao Tse-tung to Bob Dylan. A big favorite seemed to be Henry Thoreau. His "I have always been regretting that I was not as wise as the day I was born" from Walden was block-printed on a bedsheet hung over the mock-Adam fireplace at one end of the room. I remembered that from a night class at San Francisco State College, but I always figured that Henry was a bit of a nut.

Everybody in the big room seemed to be having a jolly time except for one character whose very lack of animation grabbed the eye. He was slumped in a big armchair next to the fireplace like a doll that had been hastily abandoned. Sitting down as he was, it was hard to tell how big he was, but the shoulders in a new loud sports jacket were broad and square, and the arms hanging with inert power on either side of the ornate chair looked too long for his trunk. He had enough gray in his tightly curled hair to be forty or a bit older, but his sallow face had a blank agelessness marred only by dark pockets around each expressionless, unblinking eye. He sat alone, but his thick lips were moving with sporadic twitches that should have come with sounds.

My scrutiny was broken when Matson looked up, seemed to be surprised to find me still there and grunted: "This fucking paperwork. You be okay where you are, right?"

Right. That is, until moss started growing on my north side. I was going to ask him about the big dummy in the sports jacket, when a pretty blonde in lavender came rushing up behind an impressive bosom and gasped: "Are you Joe Goodey?"

I started to admit modestly that I was, but she steam-rollered right over me: "I'm terribly sorry I've kept you wait-ing, but Mark left a message—-and I was supervising the wedding cleanup—and nobody told me that he...so I..."

I held up a kindly hand just to stop her babbling. "Never mind," I said. "You're here now. That's the impor-tant thing. Now, what?"

That stopped her a bit cold. "I don't know," she said. "Mark just said that I should meet you here and—well—show you whatever you wanted to see. What did you want to see?"

It might have seemed a bit crude to ask to be taken directly to the murderer of Katie Pierce, so I said, "Why don't we just walk around a bit. It's all new to me. You could, however, start by telling me who you are."

Several quarts of blood came rushing to her face. "Oh, I'm sorry," she said. "I'm Susan Wallstrom. I should have told you before. You must think I'm terribly rude."

"Not at all," I said. "Tell you what, Susan. Why don't you just pretend that I'm a new resident here and show me around my new home?"

She looked serious: "A straight resident, you mean?"

"I don't know. What's that?"

She blushed again, and on her it looked good. She was a bit moonfaced, but other than that she was the kind of girl they use in advertisements to lure tourists to Sweden: flax-colored hair, high cheek bones and eyes the blue of the fjords. Altogether a nice package.

"I shouldn't have said that," she said. "We're not supposed to use the word *straight* anymore. We're all just residents here, but it used to mean residents of The Institute who'd come in without...well, without social problems such as..."

"Such as shooting dope or knocking people down and taking their money?"

She didn't like that much. I got the feeling that I was just a bit too crude for her. "Well, yes," she said reluctantly, "but a lot of other problems, too."

"Like Katie Pierce's little problem with pills?"

She *really* didn't like that. Susan turned away from me and said in a muffled voice: "I'm sorry, I—Katie was a f-friend of mine. I—"

She put her hands to her face, and I could see that she was crying. Right there in the midst of everybody. Roscoe Matson didn't even look up from his paperwork. We were beginning to get a few queer looks, though, from some of the other inmates.

Good job, Joe, I told myself. You've been here nearly an hour and you're already developing a fine collection of enemies. I looked around hurriedly for some place perhaps a little less central and spotted a big set of French doors that looked as though they might lead somewhere. As gently as possible, I reached out and took Susan's arm.

"I'm sorry," I said. "Let's get out of here." She didn't protest much when I led her along the side of the room to those big doors and through them onto a small balcony overlooking the gardens. It was getting on toward late afternoon, and the shadows of the fringe of tall evergreens along the drive were reaching like long fingers to a duck pond on the edge of a redwood grove. It was starting to get a bit cool out, too.

When we got outside, she escaped my grip, moved over to the edge of the balcony and stood staring at nothing much as far as I could see.

"I am sorry," I said. "I've got this big mouth, and it sometimes runs away with my brain."

She took a deep breath of the clear, cool air and turned around. Her eyes were still on the moist side, but she had herself under control.

"No, I'm the one who should be sorry," she said. "I'm too emotional. I'm always being told that."

"It's probably not a capital crime," I said. "Did you know Katie very well?"

"I think I did," she said. "She was sort of my little sister, and for a while she worked with me in Mark's office. It's just that she was very hard not to like. Katie was so sweet and so vulnerable and..." Susan started choking up again, but then balled her fists, got a good Nordic grip on herself and shook it off. "I still can hardly believe she's dead."

"Do you know why I'm here?" I asked.

"Yes," she said, looking up into my eyes, "but I..."

"Don't you tell me I'm wasting my time, too," I said. "Try to be a bit more original. The way it's going, soon every resident of The Institute will be lined up on the lawn like a Greek chorus chanting: 'You're wasting your time, Joe Goodey, wasting your time.' Do you really think it's so impossible that somebody here could have helped Katie off the roof?"

"Yes," she said, looking up into my face, "but I think..."

Suddenly she was looking past me, not at me, and I turned to see the zombie in the horse-blanket jacket coming through the double doors with a mechanical-man shuffle.

"Tommy," she said, in a tone that seemed both affectionate and cautious at the same time. "Did you enjoy the wedding?"

A salvo of animated gibberish burst from his lips, carrying a fair amount of saliva that lightly stippled the front of Susan's pale lavender coveralls. She didn't seem to mind. The wet syllables tumbled over each other in no order that I could appreciate, but from Susan's face, he could have been telling a fascinating story. In his enthusiasm, he forgot to turn off his legs when he switched on his mouth, and Susan had to continue to back away slowly, until her back was against the cast concrete rail of the terrace.

Tommy was still shuffling forward, babbling as he went, so I stepped forward and took hold of his biceps to slow him up before he pushed Susan through the railing. It was like trying to get a grip on a moving engine piston, and I had no more effect on Tommy's forward progress than a gnat throwing itself in front of an express train.

Without thinking, I kicked him sharply behind the right knee. Anyone else would have been down on one knee wondering what hit him, but Tommy just trundled to a halt and turned to examine me with perfectly blank eyes.

Susan gave me a slightly dirty look for using such a crude method of saving her from being crushed, and said brightly, "Tommy, this is Joe Goodey, a new friend of The Institute. He came down for the wedding."

If that information didn't delight him, it didn't make him mad, either. His eyes passed over me without a ripple, and Tommy turned toward the French doors and launched himself in the direction of the living room. His lips began moving again, and nothing was coming out but a fine froth of spit. He didn't say goodbye.

"Tommy's really very harmless," Susan said, in mild reproach. "He just has to be managed very gently. He's made incredible improvement."

"I'll bet," I said, "but I imagine you've got a way to go with him."

Susan opened her mouth to answer and then shut it again.

"So there you are," said a voice behind me, and I turned to see Mark Kinsey coming through the French doors with a forced expression of bonhomie on his flabby face. "How's the tour coming along, Susan? Are you learning anything, Joe? Isn't the view from here magnificent? You ought to catch the sea views."

"Just f-fine, Mark," Susan said, a bit nervously, I thought. "I was just about to..."

"That's great," he said. "Susan's a real asset to The Institute,

Joe, even though she's been here less than a year." Before I could respond, he added: "Susan, honey, could you go give Lenore a hand in her office? I'll give Joe the seventy-five-cent tour, and we'll see you later." Susan's expression said that was all right with her, and she was soon gone with hardly a mumbled farewell to me. And just as we were becoming buddies, too.

Kinsey was as good as his word, and in the next hour or so he took me on an extensive tour of the old mansion. I saw almost everything: the vast dining room, the two kitchens, the laundry room, the Olympic-length pool in the basement flanked by sauna baths and squash courts, a billiard room with velvet drapes the color of vintage port and so much more that it was soon just a blur to me.

As we looked at each section, Kinsey praised it with the slightly spurious hyperbole of a real-estate agent working on commission. His pride in the place was evident and genuine, but his public-relations spiel tinged everything with phoniness.

"It's very nice," I said as we left the billiard room, "but I don't think I want to buy it."

Kinsey looked at me keenly until he decided that I'd made a little joke, and then gave me a pawnbroker's laugh. "Ha, ha, yes," he said, without much humor. "I guess that's about it for now. There are a lot of outbuildings, but it's getting late. You can see them tomorrow."

"I'll look forward to that," I said. "But there's one stop on the tour I think you've forgotten. We could look at that right now."

"What's that?" he asked.

"The roof terrace," I said, trying not to sound like a keen detective. "Considering why I'm here, I think that might be useful."

"Oh, sure," he said, as if glad to be reminded. "Now you'll see those sea views I told you about."

Kinsey said it was probably best to take the plush little elevator to the roof. As we stepped out, the sun lay like a fried egg on the horizon, and a crimson stain spread from it like blood. From the hills behind us to the wooded coast spreading out on both sides, calm reigned, broken only by faint, disconnected sounds from the wedding guests below. I began to understand why people went to all that trouble to get rich.

It wasn't so much a roof terrace as a natural setting for moonlight dancing, three-piece bands and the pop of champagne corks. Some pretty expensive dancing slippers had brushed over that smooth surface. The leading edge of the roof was crenelated mock-castle style, and I stood with both hands on the battlements looking at the sunset. Then I looked down to the rocky beach where they'd found Katie Pierce.

The tide was in just then; rushing water and swirling foam covered most of the rocks. But my mind's eye could still see the police photograph of Katie's battered and bloody body broken on the rocks. My mind's eye saw too damned well to suit me.

The sheriff's report said that Katie had fallen from the right-hand side of the roof. I moved over there and tried to put myself in Katie's place moments before she'd gone over the edge. I didn't like the feeling at all. I looked back at Kinsey, who seemed to be communing with some inner spirit.

I cleared my throat, startling him back to the present, and asked, "Which of the residents have access to this part of the mansion?"

He understood the question, but he said nothing for a

long moment. Then he said: "Uh, Joe, I don't think I'm the right person to answer that sort of question. Perhaps..."

"Perhaps," I said, "you didn't hear Fischer say that to me The Institute was an open book. Full cooperation, that was what the man promised. Do I have to go down and tell him that you're holding out on me?"

"Okay, okay," Kinsey said, not exactly liking that idea. "In theory, this roof, along with every other part of the mansion, is open to all residents of The Institute."

"But?"

"But, in practice, it is used only by the top echelon of members and their guests."

"That top echelon," I said, "how far down does it extend? I mean, how exclusive is it? For instance, are you among the happy elite allowed to frolic here?"

Kinsey brought his slack lips together in a way that told me that he didn't much like my style of questioning. But he couldn't think of very much he could do about it just then, so he said: "I have been here on occasion. Hugo likes to hold barbecues up here sometimes on summer evenings, and I have been invited to them."

"But you wouldn't really feel at ease sneaking up here with a girl for a little private necking?"

"No," he said judiciously. "I wouldn't do that."

"So, that cuts down the number of people who would have a legitimate reason for being up here, doesn't it?"

"Yes, it does," he answered. "But it doesn't mean that a lot of other people might not use it on the quiet. We don't lock doors here at The Institute. We have no need to."

He was probably right, and that opened my list of potential suspects right up again, and probably included some who weren't even at The Institute anymore. But then, Crenshaw wouldn't have been paying me so much money if the job had been a cinch. It would have been a lot easier for me if Kinsey had just confessed right there and then to heaving Katie over the edge and saved me a lot of trouble. Somehow I didn't think he would.

It was beginning to feel a bit pointless staying on that roof, not to mention chilly, so I suggested that we carry on with the tour. As we waited for the elevator, I asked him if Susan Wallstrom was always so jumpy and emotional.

"Not usually," he said. "I think you made her nervous, and of course she was very fond of Katie. She hasn't been with us very long, but I think she's settling in very well."

"What did she do before she came to The Institute?"

"It's hard to believe," he said, "but Susan was a guard, or whatever they call them, at the state women's prison up at Frontera. But she couldn't take the work."

Frontera. *I* knew someone at Frontera. I'd have to ask her if we had a mutual friend.

"What's the rest of today's schedule?" I asked.

"Nothing much for the next hour or so until dinner," he said. "It's a special wedding dinner for Pops Martin and Genie."

"That's the girl bride, right?"

"I believe Genie is nineteen," Kinsey said, a bit stiffly, "but she's quite old for her years."

"I'll bet," I said. "What then?"

"At about nine, we have our usual open house. Guests from the community come in for a party with the residents. The guests of honor are Pops and Genie."

"Pops Martin seems to be pretty important here," I said. "What does he do that's so special?"

"That's a bit difficult to answer," Kinsey said. "To an outsider, it might appear that Pops doesn't do much of anything. But I assure you that, next to Hugo, there's hardly a person at The Institute who has done more to help it to survive and succeed. Not even Lenore or Don Moffitt."

"Rachel told me Pops was an old-time member," I said.

"Much more than that, Joe," Kinsey said, getting a bit earnest. "Hugo and he have known each other off and on for over thirty years. They first met back in Missouri, worked on the same ships together at times and even shared a cell in prison once." The elevator arrived, and we got in.

"Sounds like a firm basis for a friendship," I said.

"But more important," Kinsey went on, "is that when Hugo was in New York City trying to get The Institute started—he was still calling it The Institute of Mankind in those days—Pops suddenly reappeared. He was drunk, just out of jail and thought the meeting was some kind of a party to crash, but when he sobered up, Pops swore that he'd help Hugo with his dream."

"Touching," I said. "So in exchange for sticking around for ten years or so, Pops Martin has a meal ticket for life." Kinsey didn't like that very much, either.

"Joe," he said, "your problem is that you're a cynic. You can't believe that The Institute could take such apparently useless material as Pops Martin and make it useful. I pity you."

"That depends," I said, "on what it uses them for. To me, Pops Martin looks just like any of the hundreds of old crooks and conmen I've seen drift in and out of jail. They usually end up in the gutter. Pops seems to have been a little luckier than most; quite a bit luckier, I'd say."

The elevator door slid open at the ground floor to reveal that same reformed character standing there with his blushing bride. That is, she was standing. He was listing heavily to port and using her for a crutch. Her hard little face did not cry out: "Use me as you will."

"Hi, Mark," Pops said. "I'm just going up for a little rest before dinner." His eyes, the color of stale beer, flicked over me, but he couldn't think of anything worth saying.

"Hi, Pops," I said. "You ought to drop in on the roof. The view is terrific up there."

As tired as he seemed to be, Pops found the energy to give me a look that you could have used to open clam shells, and he and the bride disappeared into the elevator.

8

DINNER THAT NIGHT WAS A FANCY AFFAIR, WITH Fischer and his leading lights sitting on a raised dais like the officers at a Kiwanis Club luncheon. At Fischer's side was his wife, and fanned out on either side were Rachel and Dr. Carey, Don Moffitt and a tight-lipped woman with prematurely graying hair pulled straight back from her forehead. She didn't look happy. There were a number of other faces I didn't recognize, but to my surprise at one end, looking as if he hadn't been switched on yet, was Tommy, my friend from the terrace. Sitting next to him was an overdressed, slightly imperious-looking old woman, who was giving Tommy all her attention.

Pops Martin, who looked to be a bit more rested, and Genie, got up like something that had been won at Coney Island, were sitting slightly higher in a corner of the room at a flower-decked table for two, bathed in its own personal spotlight. Fischer certainly knew how to stage an occasion.

I was seated at a long trestle table with some of the other peasants, but with a little judicious jostling I managed to sit next to Susan Wallstrom. Mark Kinsey was down the table, not looking entirely at ease, and I spotted Jack Gillette at another table. If he saw me, he kept it to himself.

While the food—the sort of wholesome institutional stuff you'd find at any third-rate hotel or a good mental hospital—was being served, I leaned on Susan to put names to some of the unknown faces at the head table. The woman with the gray hair—she couldn't have been much over thirty —turned out to be Mrs. Don Moffitt, like him an old-time resident at The Institute.

"What's she so unhappy about?" I asked Susan.

Susan really didn't like to say, being loyal and all that, but finally she whispered that she had heard that Aileen Moffitt was restless and was urging Don to leave The Institute and take a job he'd been offered back East.

"What about the guy at the end of the table who's a bit puffy around the gills? The one who looks as though he could use a stiff drink."

Susan wasn't crazy about my description, but she identified him as Harold Fischer, Hugo's cousin, who had just given up a good business in the Midwest to move into The Institute. The faded woman next to him was Mrs. Harold F. Fischer.

"What's he want to do that for?" I asked.

"Why, because he realizes that The Institute is an important social movement, and he wants to take part," Susan said, as if reading from a tract.

I let that pass. If I was going to get information from Susan Wallstrom, it wouldn't do to upset her too much. "What about the old bird sitting next to Tommy?" I asked. "The one who looks like she owns the place."

"She did own the place," Susan said, a bit smugly.

"That's Emma Carter, Tommy's mother. She's giving the mansion and the estate to The Institute."

I didn't know which little surprise to deal with first. I suppose people like Tommy have a right to have mothers, too, but you don't expect it. The other news was slightly more sensational.

"Just like that?" I said. "She's *giving* it? You mean, for free?"

"The Institute has done an awful lot for Tommy," Susan said, a little bit defensively. "Emma believes in The Institute and in Hugo," she added emphatically, "and so do I."

"That's a whole lot of belief," I said. "But what—"

Fischer started tapping on his water glass with a butter knife. It had the authoritative rat-a-tat of a machine gun, and it silenced that noisy room just as effectively. Once you could have heard a mouse fart in the big banquet room, Fischer leaned forward with the benevolent dogmatism of a man talking to obedient children.

"Good evening," he said. "If you are guests, welcome to The Institute. Welcome to our home. We are happy to have you among us. Before we get on with this evening's festivities in honor of two of our residents who got married today" —Pops and Genie in their fairy bower looked pleased with themselves—"I want to introduce you to a rather special guest." I started wondering who it was, when he said: "Mr. Joe Goodey." No one was more surprised than I was when he followed up with: "Would you stand up, Mr. Goodey so that we can all see you?"

It would have taken a stronger character than I to have resisted that command performance, so I pushed back my chair and stood up with what I hoped was lithe grace. Probably not. From where I stood, I could see almost universal puzzlement on the faces of the diners. Rachel was looking worried; Pops Martin was just beginning to enjoy himself.

Fischer, apparently a master of timing, left me dangling there long enough to encourage paranoia and make everyone wonder what the hell was going on. I was just about to sit down when Fischer said: "Mr. Goodey is a private detective from San Francisco." This revelation didn't bring smiles of welcome to many faces. A good thing, too, because they'd probably have cracked and fallen off when he added: "Mr. Goodey has come down here to try to prove that one of us killed Katie Pierce, our late sister."

Talk about the impact of the legendary turd in the punchbowl. Most of the faces that could summon up any expression at all opted for outraged hostility. It didn't look as though I was going to leave The Institute with any life-long friends. The amateur lynch mob noises continued to grow until Fischer raised a beefy hand.

In the grumbling silence that followed, he said: "Now, you and I know that Mr. Goodey is going to go away empty-handed..."

Somebody at the back of the room shouted: "And empty-headed!"

But Fischer wasn't being taken in by such cheap shots. "I say," he continued, "that we know that Mr. Goodey won't find Katie's murderer here because she wasn't murdered. But Mr. Goodey has a job to do here—it's not a job everyone would take, mind you—and I want each and every one of you to cooperate with him fully." At this, the mob at the trestle tables began their tar-and-feather-him rumbling, which only died down when Fischer raised his voice to the diamond-cutting level. "Shut up! I'm trying to say that if we all cooperate with Mr. Goodey, it won't be too long until he realizes that he's wasting his time here and goes back to San Francisco."

This was a real crowd-pleaser, and the cheers it evoked made Mrs. Carter's crystal chandeliers vibrate. I tried to look humble about the whole thing, but Fischer wasn't finished having fun yet.

"Perhaps," he said, "Mr. Goodey would like to say a few words to us."

That set off an uproar of sarcastic clapping. This was certainly turning out to be a jolly little dinner. I looked around and saw that a few people weren't clapping. Rachel, for one, was toying with her fork and looking distinctly unhappy. Mrs. Carter was spooning food off Tommy's flashy lapels and back toward his slack mouth. Jack Gillette wasn't clapping, which was interesting in itself. But, even more surprising, Pops Martin wasn't either. He was up at his table-for-two, looking preoccupied. Perhaps he was sulking because I seemed to be getting all the attention on his wedding day.

The uproar went on so long that I figured I'd have to say something just to get off the hot spot. I'd sat down during Fischer's monologue, so I got up again and stood there looking around the big room and waiting for a bit of silence. To my surprise, I got it, but I waited a little longer just to keep them on edge.

Then I said: "You're all under arrest."

That got a better laugh than it deserved from such a hostile audience, so I let it run a while and then raised my arms high like a fight referee.

"Listen," I said, glad to be able to get the message over to so many people at once, "I don't know whether Katie Pierce was murdered, much less whether someone here did it. But that's what I'm here to try to find out. You can make it easy or hard, but either way, I'm getting paid by the day, so I don't mind. Thank you."

I sat down in a pool of nearly perfect silence, but then at the edges a ripple of applause began, which grew slowly in volume until it was nearly as loud as that before I'd spoken. But this was different; it was real applause. These people obviously didn't mind being spoken to straight. If they were a lynch mob, at least they were a fair-minded lynch mob.

I enjoyed this limited approval until Fischer stopped it with an imperious gesture. "I have another announcement. The regular Saturday night open house has been canceled. Sitches will begin fifteen minutes after dinner is finished."

He started to sit down again, but a big guy at the back jumped up. "What about our guests?" he demanded. "Some of them are coming long distances to make the open house."

"To hell with them," said Fischer, not even bothering to stand all the way up. "If they are really friends of The Institute, they'll understand and come back again. If not, we don't need them." He sat down; his questioner sat down, and an excited buzz of conversation broke out all over the room.

"What are these things—these *sitches*?" I asked Susan.

"They're small meetings of about ten or twelve people," she said. "The word *sitch* is short for *situation*. As Hugo says, they're situations for intensive communication between individuals."

"What happens at these—meetings?"

"I can't describe it for you," said Susan. "You'd have to experience it yourself."

"Thanks," I said. "I think I'll give that a miss."

By this time, the banqueters were licking their sherbet spoons, and many had risen and were drifting from the dining room. Susan got up from her chair.

"I have to go now, Mr. Goodey," she said, too polite just to walk away. "I'll probably see you later."

"You probably will," I said. Then I remembered something. "Wait a minute." She stopped and looked at me with some anxiety. "Somebody told me you used to be a guard up at the ladies' slammer at Frontera," I said, "and..."

"I was a matron at the California Institute for Women at Frontera," she said with a frown.

"Okay," I said. "That's your terminology. But what I want to know is whether a girl named Irma Springler came in while you were there."

"Yes," Susan said. "Irma came in just about two weeks before I left, and I took her through orientation."

"How was she? Did she seem to have any problems? I mean, besides six long years to do?"

"No," Susan said. "Irma seemed fine when I last saw her. A bit detached, perhaps, but that's understandable. I hadn't heard of any problems when I left. Is she a friend of yours?"

"Not really," I said. "I put her there."

"It was kind of you to inquire," she said sarcastically, then shot a look at her wristwatch. "I really must be going."

It occurred to me as I watched her walk away that girls don't really look all that glamorous in coveralls, even pale mauve ones. Especially, walking away, if they're developing a bit of a lard ass.

By then, I was nearly the last one in the banquet room except for a crew of flunkies in gray who were none too joyfully clearing the tables, scraping garbage into buckets and grumbling among themselves.

This seemed like a good time to sort out my luggage in my luxury suite while the residents were having a bit of intensive communication. Upstairs, the narrow halls were deserted. When I opened the door to my room, not much had changed except that the smell of bus driver's underpants had faded somewhat. My suitcase was sitting on the hard narrow bed, as Gillette had promised. I fished out the appropriate key, unlocked the case, swung open the lid and promptly went into a cardiac arrest. The two reports —the sheriff's and Brazewell's—were no longer stacked neatly on top of my shirts where I had left them. I did a quick rummage to the bottom of the case just to make sure, then wheeled and practically ran out of the little room.

It's funny how fast you can move when you really want to. In less than a minute I was outside the big polished walnut door of Fischer's office. Gasping only slightly, I twisted the brass knob and went into the room like a rookie on his first whorehouse raid.

It was a pretty picture that greeted me. At his desk, in the light of a Tiffany-glass lamp, Hugo Fischer was leafing through Brazewell Associates' well-researched report, while back in his favorite chair like faithful dog Tray, Pops Martin was reading the sheriff's version, licking his fingers as he turned the pages. It looked like reading hour at the Old Lag's Home.

Fischer, who had put on a pair of gold-rimmed reading glasses for the exercise, looked up and raised his eyebrows as I came into the room. I thought I saw him cock an ear for the missing knock on the door. He opened his mouth, but I didn't wait to hear what would come out of it. Without breaking stride, I charged over to his desk, snatched the Brazewell Report from his hands and pivoted toward Pops Martin. The bridegroom was uncoiling as I came toward him, which brought the sheriff's report up to easy grabbing height.

"Hey," he protested, like a kid whose last comic book has been confiscated, "you can't..."

"I can, Pops," I said, facing them both. The reports were neatly tucked under my arm. "As for you, Fischer," I said, "keep your thugs out of my room and my belongings, and *your* hands off them, too."

Fischer didn't look especially disturbed to have been busted with the stolen reports. He looked up at me like a flawed Buddha. "You know, Goodey," he said, "that's a pretty libelous piece of literature you've got there. Those Brazewell people want to watch it or they'll end up in court with me on their ass."

"I don't care about that," I said. "Just keep your hands off my stuff."

I spun around and shot back out through the door. The last thing I heard before the door slammed was Fischer saying: "You already said that."

I was heading back up to my room when Roscoe Matson loomed in front of me. "Hey, Joe Goodey," he said. "I been looking all over the damn place for you. You're late."

"Late for what?"

"Your sitch, man," he said. He looked down at the clipboard he was carrying. "Let me see. Yeah, I've got you down for the Karma Room."

"Is that right?"

"That's what it says here. I don't make up the rosters. I just execute them." Matson gave me some elaborate and confusing directions how to get there and then sauntered off down the hall. I turned back toward my room, but then heard his voice. "Goodey?"

I turned around. "Yeah?"

"Just wanted to say," Matson volunteered, "that I don't like cops and I think you're barking down the wrong hole,

Ace, but you've got some balls." Before I could feel too smug about that, he added: "You may not be too bright, but, yeah, you've got guts."

"Thanks," I said.

He turned and continued down the hall with a springy athlete's walk. He probably thought he was whistling a tune.

9

MAKING A SHORT DETOUR BACK UP TO MY ROOM, I tucked the two reports under the lumpy mattress with no doubt that if Fischer wanted them back, he'd get them. There didn't seem to be a word for privacy at The Institute. I suppose I could have taped the reports under my shirt, but to tell the truth, I didn't care much whether Fischer read them. I just didn't like the way he got them.

Trying to remember Matson's directions, I backtracked through the corridors until I found myself outside a substantial green door bearing a hand-painted sign: "Karma Room." All seemed quiet inside. Squaring my shoulders, I put a hand on the doorknob and had begun to twist when from inside the room came an explosion of noise as if someone were trying to force spats onto an alligator.

I backed off a step and a half and listened intently. From my side of the door it sounded like a riot at the Tower of Babel, and it couldn't have been much quieter inside. Somehow, it didn't make me eager to charge into the Karma Room. Not just then. I called myself a coward, but the accusation didn't have much sting. I was about to turn away and go find a good, rousing game of Parcheesi, when the door to the Karma Room opened and Hugo Fischer was standing in the doorway, looking at me with benign malevolence.

"Goodey," he said, speaking over the tumult behind him. "I thought there was someone out here. Come in. You're late."

I wasn't so sure I wouldn't have preferred jumping into a snake pit, but how could I resist such a gracious invitation? Fischer turned and went back into the room as if certain that I would follow. I followed.

I walked right into a very interesting little tableau. Mrs. Donald Moffitt was leaning aggressively toward Mr. Donald Moffitt and screaming that he was a "rotten, little, chickenshit, cowardly son of a bitch." That wasn't bad for openers, and Moffitt just sat there in an overstuffed chair and took it.

I paused for a moment, not wanting to interrupt this earnest communication, but quite willing to hear a bit more of it. No chance. Ten or twelve pairs of eyes swiveled toward me as one. From most of the expressions, I felt as welcome as a rustler at the cowboy's ball. But then Rachel Schute spoke up to say: "Sit down, Joe. Just take any empty seat."

They were seated in an irregular circle on a couple of small couches, some easy chairs and a piano bench. I took the least conspicuous seat I could find, between Aileen Moffitt and the great man's cousin Harold. Further to my right were the new Mrs. Pops Martin, Dr. James Carey and Mark Kinsey. To the left were Don Moffitt, Susan Wall-strom and Rachel. Directly across from me, Fischer regained his lordly armchair, flanked on either side by Pops Martin and Cousin Harold's harmless-looking wife. Most of the power structure was there.

Moffitt was looking pretty relieved to have the pressure off him for a moment, but then Harold Fischer stuck out his mock-Hugo jaw and said: "Well, Don, is what Aileen says true? Are you the original nutless wonder? Are you afraid to have a go in the big cold world outside? That job offer in New York sounds pretty good to me. What's holding you back?"

Though only a cousin, up close Harold looked enough like Hugo to be his brother. They were like two pots that had been uniform when put into the kiln, but which came out different. Where Hugo was flawed, dynamic and unique, Harold was symmetrical, inert and very ordinary, a poor facsimile.

"Fuck you, Harold," Don Moffitt snarled. "You've no room to talk. If it's so wonderful out there, why aren't you still in Omaha selling used cars? Instead of here in The Institute holding on to Hugo's shirttails for all you're worth."

Score one for counterpunching. Harold's handsome face developed a red blotch as if Moffit had landed a stinging jab. "Listen," Harold said. "I was out there for twenty-five years. Some might even say I did all right. I sold the Cadillac dealership because I felt that The Institute offered more. I..."

"He's right, Don," James Carey cut in with authority. "Selling cars may be only a little better than pimping"— Harold's face got a little bit redder—"but Harold made his thirty grand a year, maybe more. And he made it in the market place, where there's no nice cushion under your ass if you fall. What the hell have you ever done in the real world but hustle drugs, knock over filling stations and generally fuck up your life?"

From Moffitt's expression I could tell that the contest

had changed, and not so subtly either. I had a feeling that he could handle his yapping wife and this poor imitation of Hugo, but in Jim Carey he was up against something else—a peer, and worse, a rival. He inhaled sharply as if to gather momentum.

"Bullshit!" he snapped, leaning toward Carey aggressively like a stag eager to lock horns. "You're operating under some bullshit false assumption, Carey, that I want to leave The Institute but am afraid to."

"That's what it looks..." Carey began mildly enough.

"Well," Moffitt continued, his ball bearing eyes sweeping the assembled company, "let me tell you—let me tell you all unequivocally—that I don't want to leave The Institute, and I'm not going to leave The Institute—now or ever, not willingly." He turned toward Aileen, who was watching his face with intensity. "It's my wife who wants to leave," he told the group, "so that she can have a house all her very own and all the horseshit modern conveniences every housewife in America has. And the two-car garage. The whole bit." He leaned even further toward his wife, as if he were going to spring at her throat. "Well," he said, gritting his gray, irregular teeth, "if that's what my asshole wife wants, she can just go get it without me. Anytime she likes. I'm staying!"

Under this verbal assault, Aileen Moffitt crumbled. She didn't cry, but her eyes, already suspiciously moist, went a bit vacant, and her thin lower lip began to tremble. Almost unconsciously, she put both balled fists to her temples, looked wildly around the room as if surrounded by a hanging jury, and then jumped up from her chair and ran to the door. After a bit of trouble with the knob, she wrenched it open and fled, leaving the door open a crack behind her.

Christ! This was better than tag-team wrestling. They

certainly didn't play by girls' rules around here. I was wondering when somebody was going to pull a knife when a voice said: "Well, what have you got to say for yourself, asshole?"

I looked around to find out who the asshole was, and it turned out to be me. Mrs. Harold F. Fischer was leaning halfway out of her comfy chair and pointing a mauve finger-nail in my direction. And I always thought she was such a nice little woman.

'Me?" I said, as if there was some room for doubt.

"Yes you, sucker," screamed Pops Martin's brand-new bride, going into a Bela Lugosi impression. "We're talking to you. Explain yourself!"

"Well," I said modestly, "I'm just doing my job, just noodling around down here trying to serve the cause of justice and the common good. Trying to..."

"Not that crap, you lame motherfucker," cried dear, gentle Susan Wallstrom. "We're talking about the game you've been running on Rachel for the last year."

"Game?" I said in a voice that came out in an unfortunately girlish falsetto. But I had the merest inkling what they were talking about. Somebody had obviously been telling stories. Not that I cared to discuss it at that moment, of course. I was there on business.

"Don't try that horseshit on us, you chauvinist prick," Susan insisted, puffing up like a Valkyrie. "You know what we're talking about. You go over to Rachel's, eat her food, drink her booze, play with her emotions and then split without leveling with her, you jerk."

Then all the women in the room were on me except Rachel, who seemed to be memorizing the carpet. Harold Fischer and Don Moffitt were laying back on the oars, seemingly quite content to let me get cut up by these amazons.

Hugo Fischer was playing the paterfamilias and keeping his hands clean.

I sat there feeling like one of Genghis Khan's boys being raped by a nun. I don't ordinarily mind being called a whole bagful of motherfuckers; it's part of life. But for these ladies to ratpack me before I even knew the rules of the game seemed a bit unfair. Apparently, in the sitch, anything went, up to and including character assassination and lies, but the action stopped just short of blunt instruments.

But even my fabled tolerance had begun to wear a bit thin when the yapping died down a little and Susan said: "What about you, Rachel? You just sit there while we badmouth Joe. You've moaned enough about the way he's treated you, but now that he's here in a sitch with you, you've got nothing to say. Is that right?"

The room fell silent while we all looked at the top of Rachel's head. Then she did just what I'd hoped she wasn't going to do. She raised her head until her eyes met mine. They were pale eyes to begin with, a delicate astral blue, and now they were nearly opaque as they pinned me to my chair.

I tried to think of an urgent appointment that would get me out of the Karma Room, but before I could, Rachel said: "It's true, Joe. You've messed me up quite a bit in the last year, coming around, going away, then showing up again, but with no commitment at all. Do you think you've been fair to me?"

I had no desire to look Rachel manfully in the eye at that particular moment so I was able to notice that Dr. James Carey was following the confrontation with a particular intensity. I could see that he might have a special interest in its outcome.

It was really more of a monologue than a conversation

up to that point, but I knew I had to say something. I supposed I could have pretended to faint, but that mob would have probably tied me upright in my chair and carried on.

"What do you mean?" I said, just to stall a bit.

"You know what I mean, Joe," Rachel said, warming to the job. "You've just been using me when it was convenient to you. Sure, it was comfortable to come over and see me, play with the kids, stay the night. You knew I liked you a lot, so it was good for your ego. But what was there in it for me?"

"Look, Rachel," I said defensively, "I never promised..."

"Don't be so chickenshit," cut in Genie Martin with a sneer.

"Be honest, Joe," said Susan. "Tell the truth. That's what the sitch is for."

To be completely frank, that's not exactly what I had come to The Institute to do. Not that I'm particularly dishonest. I mean, no more than the average private investigator. But I'd have rather faced a punk with a .38 in each hand than tell Rachel the truth. But that was exactly what these virtual strangers—and Rachel—were waiting for me to do.

To my own surprise, I heard my voice say: "All right, Rachel, I'll level with you. There is no future for you and me. It's just no good, it wouldn't work."

She seemed to take it well enough. No tears, no overt emotion. She even smiled drily, which, I thought, was a fine reaction for a woman being given the finger, even in a super-polite and sincere manner. I sat back, relieved that it was over. That hadn't been so bad. I ought to try telling the truth more often. It could get to be fun.

"Why, Joe?" Rachel asked quietly, but it certainly shocked me. "Go the whole way for once."

Why? What did she mean, *why*? Women didn't ask the reasons why they'd been dumped. Not in the circles I traveled in. This was asking too much.

"Look..." I said.

"Answer her, scumbag!" screamed Genie. Someone was really going to have to talk to that girl about her mouth. Somebody was going to mistake it for a sewer one of these days. Maybe her mother didn't tell her that nice boys don't date foulmouthed broads more than once.

"The reasons can't be that terrible," chimed in Mother Fischer. "You owe it to Rachel to level with her. We won't bite you."

That I could believe. But not much else. Then I thought: what the hell, why not? They could kill me, but they couldn't eat me. Cannibalism is illegal. Rachel was asking for it; maybe she should get it.

"You're going to laugh," I warned them.

"Try us, Joe," said Rachel. "We could use a good laugh."

"Okay." I took a deep breath. "Rachel," I said. "There are two reasons why I can't make it with you."

Rachel just nodded her head and kept her eyes on my face.

"Well," I said, still trying to think for some way to stall but failing, "the first reason is that you're too rich. You've just got too much money."

The room exploded. Everybody fell about in their seats laughing. At me. They roared, they giggled, they gasped for breath. Somebody in the Karma Room had the makings of a great comedian. Very funny. Except to me. I just sat there waiting for the general merriment to die down and hoping that I could buy them off with that tidbit of home truth. Gradually, the laughter died down.

"What else, Joe?" Rachel asked. "What's the other reason?"

All right. I was getting a bit tired of this bullshit. If I was going to start telling the truth, I might as well jump in with both boots.

"Rachel," I said, trying to take as much sting out of it as I could with the tone of my voice, "you're just too old for me. I'm sorry."

Silence. Deep, dark, aboriginal silence. Nobody had a thing to say. To my surprise, the expression on Rachel's face hadn't changed much. If it was a mortal blow, she was taking it like a stoic. She looked relieved, and I don't think what I'd said had been as much of a surprise to her as I'd thought it would be. I was glad. I was also astonished at myself. The Institute must have really had something going for it. I'd only been around the place about ten hours, and I was already being honest.

I had a feeling that the primeval silence was going to break any second, and that one of our jolly little party wasn't going to be the better off for it. God knows, I didn't have much more to say, but I could imagine that the others might think of something.

Just then, Hugo Fischer's barking baritone broke the silence. To my surprise and relief, he was talking not to me but to Dr. James Carey. Fischer accused the good doctor of spending too much time up in Sausalito wooing Rachel and not enough time doing his job at The Institute.

Slowly, deliberately, like a craftsman who really loved his job, Fischer took Carey apart verbally. He had a gift for it, all right. The others joined in with contrapuntal low blows that soon had Carey scrambling for cover.

Carey tried to defend himself, but he couldn't very well maintain that in courting the Widow Schute he was really serving The Institute's interests. Not with Rachel there, anyway. Finally, he gave up defense entirely, like an arm-weary heavyweight hanging on the ropes absorbing punishment, until the rest of them got bored and turned to someone else.

This someone else was Susan Wallstrom. But to my surprise, the mob, led by Fischer, didn't harangue her, but instead softly and tenderly led Susan to examine her problem, which was in the boy-girl area, to put it politely. It seemed that, despite his dopey appearance, Mark Kinsey was pawing the earth in his eagerness to get young Susan into the sack. Susan couldn't quite see her way clear, although she claimed she really wanted to.

It was a different Fischer I saw talking to Susan. Gone was the scowling martinet, the little tin god who knew he was firmly in control of the lives of a bunch of children and mental incompetents. Instead, Fischer was the gentle counselor, all-knowing, all-loving, all-forgiving, and very believable in the role. All else was forgotten except Susan's problem, and Fischer took it upon himself to try to put it right. The others chimed in occasionally, but it was Fischer who carried the weight, and he did a good job of it. Susan didn't instantly stand up and throw off her sexual hang-ups, but she did seem to feel better, and it was obvious that she gave Fischer the credit. When she looked at him, her eyes glowed with near reverence.

But just in case his kindly treatment of Susan had given the others ideas above their station, Fischer slipped on the four-ounce gloves and worked each of the others over as if they were a series of punching bags. It was quite impressive, in a sadistic sort of way.

Fischer started with Mark Kinsey, portraying him as an infantile satyr who didn't have the human decency or compassion to allow Susan to discover how she really felt about him before trying to slip his horny hand into her undies. I had to give Fischer credit. If he could transform Kinsey into Don Juan Casanova, he was a magician.

Next was Cousin Harold. Fischer denounced him for going around bragging about his hotshot Cadillac agency when in reality he was a broken-down used car hustler who was damned lucky to have gotten into The Institute before the police or the Internal Revenue Service got him. Harold, he suggested, would be a lot better off to emulate the behavior of The Institute's ex-addicts and forget about his sordid past. Then on to Rachel. Fischer dealt with her a bit more lightly than he had the residents, but he put on his Chief Thundercloud face when he accused her of playing the dilettante, dipping into The Institute but then running back to her luxurious life in Sausalito. Rachel, Fischer said, had better make up her mind which world she wanted. "You'd better," he cautioned her, not unkindly, "shit or get off the pot, little lady." Not eloquent perhaps, but to the point.

Fischer looked around the room to see if there were anybody left unwounded. He seemed satisfied that he'd made the rounds but then spotted Mrs. Cousin Harold—I never did find out if she had a first name—sheltering behind a massive, motherly bosom. Almost as an afterthought, he advised her to "stop wandering through the halls like Lady Macbeth wringing your hands and mourning the loss of your 20-cubic-foot freezer, Axminster wall-to-wall carpeting and Wednesday afternoon Mahjong orgies." Mrs. Harold agitated her wattles, willing to admit to any sin just to get off the hot-spot.

I noticed that Fischer had passed right over Pops and Genie. Perhaps it was just as well. Pops was nodding in his chair, nearly asleep, and Genie didn't look in the mood for serious introspection. If anything, she looked a bit apprehensive, but somehow I didn't think it was a case of virgin's jitters.

Apparently sated, Fischer heaved himself out of his armchair and announced: "Well, I suppose we'd better go join the others in..."

I never did learn where they were going to join the others, because I was up and out of the door in record time. I wasn't eager to look Rachel in the eye in the immediate future, and there seemed no better time to take a little walk. I was halfway down the hall when they followed me out of the room like passengers leaving a crowded subway, all together yet beginning to break into ones and twos.

I heard a voice behind me call: "Joe."

It was Rachel's voice, and I kept going.

10

Without actually running, I moved away from the Karma Room as quickly as possible. A convenient flight of stairs led down to the ground floor and a side door out into the cool darkness surrounding the big building. After a few minutes, it wasn't so dark. The stars were bright in a clear sky, and a gibbous moon was doing its best. The rich scent of flowering manzanita hung lightly on the soft breeze.

Behind me, the sound of chattering voices was rising, but as far as I could see I was the only one at large. I began to move away from the side of the building toward the big front lawn where the wedding had been held that afternoon. But then out of the darkness at the far edge of the lawn came two figures in gray overalls with white armbands moving with the traditional measured pace of a security patrol. They were walking with their heads together, one tall and white, with hollow, sucked-in cheeks, the other shorter, black and gesturing with barely concealed agitation.

For no particular reason, I ducked into the shadows to

wait until they passed. I suppose I could have danced out into the moonlight, introduced myself and inquired of their health, but there was something about The Institute that was already turning me into a lurker. So I stayed there, enjoying the darkness, until they'd passed—the big one moaning about some grave injustice, the little one chiming in with a chorus of: "Yeah, but bullshit, man..."

Once they'd disappeared around the side of the mansion, I straightened up and stealthily made my way along the edge of the lawn, keeping well in the dark patches, until I was able to reach the orderly grove of cypress pines at the far end. From there I admired the mansion aglow with light.

I strained my ears, but couldn't hear a thing from the mansion. The only sound in the night was the rushing of the waves against the rocks and the occasional distressed night bird. Now what, Goodey? I asked myself. You don't particularly want to talk to Rachel Schute right now, but what are you doing out here? How is this going to help Fred Crenshaw?

No answer. I turned away from the mansion, and something deeper in the trees caught my eye. I blinked and it was gone. Then it was there again—a spectral figure with a flash of white. That was either a ghost, or somebody was out there whom I hadn't yet met. I like making new friends, so I started moving away from the mansion and the sea, my eyes searching for the specter. I saw it again, but then lost it, and soon I found that I was following a faint path taking me in a northerly direction along the coast, rather than away from it.

What's more, I was climbing, as my protesting legs and lungs began to tell me, and the ground underfoot was getting rockier. The trees were thinning, too, and eventually there were more rocks, even boulders, than trees. The moon over the sea was on my left now, peeping at me through diminishing foliage. Then the trail jogged to the left, and I came out onto a clearing at the edge of a cliff overlooking the sea, the rocks and the mansion tucked neatly below among the breaking surf. From the edge I could see most of the terrace from which Katie Pierce had taken her big fall.

There was a sound to my right, and when I turned to investigate, something hit me behind the left ear, and the starry heavens began to fold in over my head like a collapsing tent. The rocky ground rose up to meet me.

When I opened my eyes, the stars were gone. They'd been replaced by a Fourth of July fireworks exhibition on the inside of my skull. I tried to raise my hands to ward off the rockets but found that they were tied behind my back. I tugged as hard as I was able, but only succeeded in giving my legs, which seemed to be up behind my shoulder blades, a painful wrench. Uh oh. A still, small voice told me that someone had hogtied me. And done a professional job of it, too.

I swiveled my head to the left, removing a few useless layers of skin, and found that someone was looking at me with a gleeful expression. In the dim, dim light of an oil lamp behind him, all I could see was a demonic grin, a pair of glittering eyes and an exuberant white beard that seemed to be full of electricity. My phantom.

"So you're awake, are you, you son of a bitch?" he said.

"I think, you've made a little mistake, sir," I said. I make it a practice always to be polite to people who have me hogtied. It works out better that way.

"*Noooo*," he brayed. "It's you who's made the mistake, sonny. And now you're going to pay for it. I warned you bastards not to mess with J. B. Carter, and now I've got one of you. Yes sir, I've got you."

J. B. Carter. Wheels began to whir, and cogs clicked neatly into place. Mrs. J. B. Carter's J. B. Carter. I'd sort of wondered whether there was one or whether Mrs. C. was just one of those batty old widows who can't wait to give away her all to the first swami who comes along.

"You've got me all right," I said, "but I think you've got me out of season. What did you use—a sledgehammer?"

"No, sir," he cackled meanly. "This!" He hefted something oblong into view and smacked it into his other palm with a nasty *whump*. It was a sock—an argyle sock—stuffed with sand, and impressive in a silly way. He stuck his home-made mule-stunner under my nose, and it occurred to me that the only thing worse than being hit with a sock full of sand was being hit with a dirty sock full of sand. In fact, I didn't much like pointing the finger of suspicion—couldn't, in fact—but one of us was enjoying a serious case of B.O.

"Uh, nice," I said. "Very nice." The back of my head throbbed in unison with every word. "But I think I can clear up a certain misunderstanding here. You think I am a resident of The Institute. Is that correct?"

"I know you're one of those claim-jumping sons-a-bitches," he said, slapping Old Sockdolager into his palm again. "You're not fooling me."

"I'm not trying to," I said, a bit testily. You try holding an extended conversation lying on your stomach with your hands and feet tied together behind your back, rocking horse-style.

"Could you do me a favor, Mr. Carter?"

"What's that?" he said suspiciously.

"Just reach into my right hip pocket and take out my wallet."

"I'm not a thief!" he said haughtily, as if a pickpocket were a notch lower than a blackjack mechanic.

"I just want you to have a look at my identification," I said patiently. "That's all. I think it will prove to you that I'm not with The Institute. In fact, I'm investigating The Institute."

"Investigating?" he said, reaching for my back pocket. At least I had him curious. "Hell!" he grunted. "I can't see a damned thing in this cave." He reached somewhere and came out with a tiny, key-chain flashlight. A little beam of light lit up the papers in his hand. Carter fumbled in a shirt pocket and came out with a pair of round steel-rimmed glasses. With these on his nose, he started browsing seriously.

"Jonah Webster Goodey, eh?"

"That's right."

"Funny name, Jonah," he said. "Means bad luck or something like that, doesn't it?"

"Something like that," I said. "Some say it's an old Indian name meaning He-Who-Should-Be-Untied."

That didn't strike him as very amusing, so he just grunted and kept reading. He wasn't a speed reader.

"Private investigator?" he said, as if it weren't written right in front of his nose.

"That's right, Mr. Carter," I said patiently. "I used to be a policeman."

"That don't mean you're not with them bastards," he said. "They've got cops. They've got a big shot from the sheriff's department in their pocket, and that's why I haven't had any success against them."

"Look," I said, truly getting weary, "I don't work for The Institute. I'm trying to find out who killed Katie Pierce."

At Katie's name, Carter stopped reading and looked

directly at me. With that little flashlight under his chin, I could see his face better, and some of the glitter seemed to have gone out of his eyes. I couldn't see much of his expression through that bush on his face, but when he spoke, his voice was softer, somehow older.

"Katie?" he said. "I'll tell you who killed Katie. That mealy-mouthed faker down there in my house, that's who. Hugo Fischer!"

Now, that was an interesting theory that I'd be interested in pursuing a bit further, but preferably from a vertical position. Maybe this old geezer would turn out to be useful.

"Can you prove that?" I asked, but he ignored the question. Carter had gotten up from his crouching position and stood looking down at me.

"If you're not with The Institute," he asked, "who do you work for?"

"Frederick M. Crenshaw," I said. "Katie's grandfather. Now will you untie me, for Christ's sake? I'm beginning to turn to stone."

Carter stuck his hand into his beard, probably to stroke his chin, and looked doubtful. Then he made a decision. "All right," he said. "I'll take a chance." Reaching into a side pocket, he unlimbered a menacing looking bowie knife and knelt down again. I couldn't see exactly what he was doing, but hoped that galloping senility hadn't made his hand shake too much. Suddenly, my feet and hands were freed from each other.

Finally, he stood up with the rope in his hands, but I still lay there waiting for life to return to my limbs. Slowly and painfully it did, and I accepted the hand he offered me and got to my still-numb feet. I had to remain hunched because the ceiling of the cave was about six inches shorter than I was.

"Sorry about that," he said. "I'd have sworn you were one of them. I wondered why you weren't wearing one of them colorful outfits, but then I figured maybe you were some sort of plainclothes night-fighter out to get me."

I shook the fizzy feeling out of my hands, and as soon as I thought I could trust my legs, I said: "Do you think we could go outside, Mr. Carter? It's a bit—uh—close in here."

He looked a bit sheepish, handed my wallet to me and led me out of the cave. As I followed him, I could see that he'd made a sort of bed in one corner and had a little store of pots and pans and other utensils. A pair of binoculars hung on the wall.

The air was a lot less funky outside, and I stood erect and took several deep breaths. It felt good. We were standing only about ten feet back from the edge of the cliff where I'd become acquainted with Carter's sock full of sand. I stood looking out to sea while behind me Carter was fussing with the foliage we'd had to pass through to get out of the cave. He panted audibly, as if struggling with something.

I waited, then got impatient, and asked him: "Mr. Carter, what the hell do you think you're doing?"

"Fixing up the entrance to my cave," he said, giving the greenery a final adjustment. "Those dope fiends would give anything to find this place. They'd be up here after me with flame throwers."

"No, I mean what are you doing up here living like a caveman, while Mrs. Carter is down there in your mansion, sitting at Hugo Fischer's feet? At least you say it's yours. The people at The Institute seem to think your wife is giving it to them."

What I could see of his expression was pretty sour. Carter looked up at me and said: "Goodey, if you know anything about the state of California's community-property law, you know that according to the idiots who run things, everything that is mine is half Emma's."

"Yes," I said. "I've heard rumors to that effect." Fortunately when my ex-wife, Patricia Berkowitz Goodey, had divorced me the year before, there'd been no property to share. And she'd been so relieved to get rid of me that she wouldn't have bothered if there had been.

"Well," Carter said, "the fact that I spent my life grubbing a fortune out of the mountains of Nevada with these"—he held up a pair of gnarled hands—"didn't matter when Emma fell under Fischer's spell and decided that we ought to give the damned place to The Institute."

"But you weren't crazy about that idea?" I asked.

"Not a bit," he said feistily. "I could see through that phony messiah from the beginning."

"Your wife and the others down there seem to think it's done your son, Tommy, a lot of good," I said.

That slowed him down a bit. "So you saw Tommy, did you?" he said, his face seeming to soften.

"Yes," I said. "But only briefly. What about you? Don't you agree that The Institute has helped him?"

Carter thought about that one. At last he said: "I don't rightly know. I really don't." He seemed to be struggling to be fair. "I have to admit that he's not in that nut house anymore. That's something."

"What's wrong with him?" I asked.

"You tell me," Carter snapped. "I've been asking myself that for forty years. He was as pretty a little boy as you ever saw. Bright as a button, he was. You never saw such a lad. Then when he was six years old he took sick. Fever. I don't know. I was away in the mountains—prospecting. When I came back, he was gone, and a little animal was left in his place. Half the time he was rolled up in a ball like a hibernating raccoon, and then like lightning he was climbing the walls like a monkey and trying to rip the place—and himself —apart. In the end, we had to have him put away. It near broke Emma's heart."

"But then Hugo and The Institute came along," I said, giving him a touch of the spur.

"Yeah," J.B. said reflectively. "And a couple of years ago Hugo talked Emma into bringing the boy—what was left of him—home. It's not the first time Tommy's been back with us, you know. Happened several times, but every time he had to go back. He'd seem to improve, but then he'd get so wild that we'd have to send him back. He's strong as an animal, you know."

"I got that feeling," I said. "Do you think he's improved since he's been home this time?"

Carter was thoughtful. "Yes, I'll give them that much. But he could go bad again any day. I wouldn't trust Hugo if he walked from here to Japan and tap-danced back. After he tried and failed to 'sell me the dream,' as he puts it, he fell back to the idea that if Emma and I only signed the place over to him, Tommy would have a nice, safe home for life. Good deal, eh?"

"I've heard better," I said. "What happened?"

"Well, as I said, I played along until this big signing-over ceremony down at the house. They made a real festive occasion out of it. A couple of tame movie stars hailed up from Los Angeles, people from the newspapers, that noisy goddamned band blaring away. Everything but a three-ring circus and the pope to give his blessing. Say," he said, peering at me keenly, "you're not Catholic, are you?"

"Not this year," I said. "Then what?"

"Well, it was all mighty festive. Fischer was grinning like a mule eating sweet corn through a barbwire fence. Everybody gathers around that oval oak table in the big living room, Fischer gives Emma a fountain pen, and she dutifully signs the contract, simpering like a ninny. Then he hands the pen to me. But I surprised him a little. I took that contract, ripped it in about a million pieces and would have shoved it down his fat throat if a couple of his thugs hadn't grabbed me. It was quite a hoo-ha, I can tell you. I thought Fischer was going to have a stroke."

"When was this?" I asked.

"Last October."

"And that's when you took to this cave, and started playing hide and seek?"

"No," he said. "That was a bit later. After his pretty ceremony was ruined, Fischer threw out all the outsiders, beat his chest and howled like a scalded baboon. And everybody else looked at me as though I'd sat on the birthday cake. But then pretty soon he calmed down a little, and called a megathon."

"What's that?" I asked.

"Sorry," the old man said. "When you're around The Institute for any time you start using the same gibberish they do. A *megathon* is sort of a long meeting of the big shots of The Institute, which gives Hugo Fischer an opportunity to rant and rave and howl for as long as he likes. Some of them have gone on for a week, day and night. Usually he calls them when he wants to straighten somebody out who's threatening to throw a monkey wrench into Fischer's master plan to rule the world."

"And in this case," I said, "that was you."

"Yep, that was me, all right. Only for the first few hours,

you wouldn't have known I was there. Fischer started out taking names and kicking asses among the faithful, sorting out internal feuds, putting down minor rebellions and just enjoying making his pet animals crawl around on their bellies."

"Sounds like good clean fun," I said. "But I imagine that Fischer got around to you eventually."

"Oh, he did that, sure enough. After about eighteen hours straight, when we're all supposed to be about on the ropes, Fischer turned loose his dogs—Moffitt, Jim Carey, Pops Martin, the whole bunch—on me. They really ripped up the floorboards and went after me. I was an ungrateful old bastard; I was standing in the way of great human progress; I was condemning my own son to life in a strait jacket. Then, Fischer pushed Emma's button, and she lit out after me, drawing on over fifty years of ups and downs and sideways. When she was done, there was nothing left you could call me. She didn't miss a stop. She ended up screaming that she hated me because I was causing so much pain and trouble to this great, decent, beautiful man—she was talking about Fischer, mind you."

"I figured as much."

"Well, about this time I was supposed to melt into a great big puddle of remorse. They were all prepared to leap up and embrace me as a brother once I'd admitted the error of my ways. I just waited until Emma had finally wound down to a quiet boohoo, stood up and walked right out of there. I haven't talked to any of them since."

"What have you been doing all this time? Not hiding in that dinky cave?"

"Some of the time," he said cagily, "but I've got a dozen places on this estate where I could hide out from an army. If

I hadn't decided to find you tonight, you'd never have found me."

I rubbed the back of my head and admitted that he was probably right. "But is it really necessary for you to do all this hide-and-seek stuff?"

He looked a bit put out at the question. "Hugo Fischer is never going to drive me off my own land. I'll outlast them. I'll still be here when every last one of those drug-crazed maniacs and bloodsuckers is out on the highway, even if Emma goes with them."

"You probably will," I agreed, "but is all the hiding and commando stuff necessary? You don't really think Fischer or anyone else from The Institute would hurt you? I seem to recall that they believe in nonviolence."

Carter cocked an eye at me like a cunning old bird. "No, Goodey," he said. "I don't believe Fischer would. Not him. But not all of his flunkies are so choosy about high ideals. So, just to be on the safe side, I keep moving."

"I can see your point," I said, "but..."

Just at that moment, we both heard voices. They were coming in our direction. Suddenly, Carter was as alert as a jack rabbit.

"I'm gone," he said, and started moving toward the bushes.

"Wait," I said, grabbing his arm. It was thin, but tough and sinewy. "I've got some more questions. How can I find you?"

"You can't," he said, jerking out of my grip easily. "If I want to talk to you, I'll do the finding. If you come looking for me, you'd better be mighty careful." Then he was gone like a wisp of smoke.

I walked back over toward the edge of the cliff and tried to look casual. The voices got louder, and in less than a minute, the two security guards I'd dodged down below came out of the trees to the little clearing.

They didn't look friendly. It may have been my imagination, but I thought the little one got a better grip on the sawed-off baseball bat he was carrying.

"What are you doing up here, Mr. Goodey?" he asked.

"Oh, just admiring the view," I said carelessly. "Why do you want to know?"

That wasn't the answer he'd been looking for, but he said: "Security is very important here at The Institute. We have enemies. We like to know just what's going on at all times on our property."

"Oh," I said innocently. "In that case, I suppose it won't hurt to tell you that I was talking with a friend."

"A friend." They were surprised.

"Who's that?" demanded the big one.

"Just a friend," I said. "He lives"—I made a vague gesture up toward the woods—"out there someplace."

"In the woods?"

"Uh huh."

"J.B.," said the taller one. "This guy's been talking to that old bastard, Carter." He turned back to me. "Where'd you see him?"

"Around," I said. "But he's gone now. He said he had to go to see a man about buying some dynamite." They both looked startled, then realized that I was putting them on.

"He belongs in a loony bin!" exclaimed the tall one. "He's nothing but an old..."

But the other guard was tugging him away from me along the cliff's edge. I wished them a lot of luck trying to find J.B.

"I'll keep that in mind," I said as they walked away

rapidly. "Look out for his sock." They disappeared into the woods.

The mansion was dark and deserted when I got back to it, and nobody challenged me as I crept up the stairs to my room. I opened the door and was groping for the light switch, when a girl's voice said: "Don't turn on the light."

11

I PEEKED WARILY AROUND THE DOOR AND FOUND GENIE Martin looking at me from the bed. My bed. The pink coveralls were gone, and a sheer silk nightgown didn't hide the fact that she was stripped for action. She was sitting propped up against the pillows, and the expression on her face was probably meant to be seductive. Instead of removing her make-up for bed, she'd obviously added more and none too subtly. Her heavily kohled eyes made her look like a raccoon in heat.

"Hello," I said, never at a loss for an original opening, "aren't you in the wrong room?"

"I hope not," Genie said, switching on the bedside lamp. "You'd better close the door or we're likely to have more company."

"Like who?" I said, taking her advice. "Pops?" But I felt better with the door closed.

She snorted prettily, showing a nice set of sharp little teeth that didn't do anything to dispel the raccoon impression. "Not a chance. The great lover is upstairs practicing breathing through his mouth. You never heard anything like it. Did you know that he keeps his teeth in a glass of water by the side of the bed? Ugh!"

She shuddered like a small girl who'd just been offered a fresh worm, and I felt a pang of compassion for the old hoodlum. I also got a vivid mental image of him snoring wet-mouthed at the ceiling. Not a pretty picture.

"You must have had some idea what you were marrying," I said, looking around for someplace to sit. There was a chair at the table, and I reached for it.

"That's easy for you to say," she said spitefully. She patted what little bed she had to spare. "Sit over here by me."

It was a tempting offer, but I said: "No thanks, not on the first date." I turned the chair around and straddled it, facing Genie. "You didn't say what you were doing here," I reminded her.

"Waiting for you." I'll give her credit; she said it without coquetry. But somehow I didn't feel flattered.

"Why me?"

"Who else?" she said, almost bitterly. "What am I going to do, go crawl into bed with Hugo? Or maybe that asshole Kinsey? Listen, these people think Pops Martin is pretty hot shit around here. He's the Grand Old Man, Hugo's right arm. If I so much as batted an eye at any of the guys in The Institute, they'd break both legs copping out on me. Most of them are eunuchs, anyway. I doubt if they could come up with one good hard-on between the bunch of them."

If I'd wanted straight talk, I'd come to the right place. Genie didn't waste much time on circumlocution. "If that's what you were looking for, why marry Pops?" I asked. "You don't look like a girl who would be short of candidates."

She shrugged, dropping the neckline of her nightie another inch down her breasts. If it was calculated, it was a nice move. "I didn't get a better offer," she said. She must not have liked the expression in my eyes because she added: "Do you know what they had me doing here? Washing dishes. Then waiting on tables. That sort of dreck. As Genie Robbins, I was strictly another pair of hands. As Mrs. Pops Martin, I don't wash dishes. I've got status. I drive that Thunderbird Hugo gave him, and everyone kisses my ass. Does that sound like a bad deal, to you?"

"Not that part of it, maybe," I said, "but if you're up here tonight, what are you going to do all the other nights?"

"I'll manage," she said. I must have looked doubtful. "Christ," she added explosively, "tonight was special. You know, I was a princess today. A fucking princess."

"You looked like a princess," I said, without stretching the truth too much. Who says there can't be hard-faced princesses with eyes older than time?

"It was beautiful," she said. A bit of glow came into her flinty eyes, and she looked even younger. "Did you see the ceremony on the lawn?"

"Yeah, it was very impressive," I said.

"Impressive?" she said indignantly. "It was wonderful—beautiful. And you saw us at dinner all by ourselves at that special table. Did you ever see so many flowers? And maybe you noticed that Hugo didn't give us any shit at the sitch. Not us. Not tonight. Then after the sitch, we went up to Pops' apartment. He put on a very romantic record, and I went into the bathroom—a *private* bathroom, all to ourselves!—to put on this." She fingered the sheer material of her nightgown lovingly. "I splashed on my best perfume —twenty bucks an ounce—and came back out into the bedroom. Do you know what I found?"

"You tell me."

"Him!" She spat out the word like a bad taste. "Sound

asleep in the bed—snoring—and with no teeth in! Do you blame me for coming up here?"

"I don't," I said. "But Pops might if he finds out."

"He won't."

"You know him better than I do," I shrugged. "But you can't know him all that well if tonight was a big surprise to you. I don't want to be gross, but there must have been some engagement period."

"Huh?" She was puzzled, but then it dawned on her what I was getting at. She got a bit shrill: "Are you kidding? I never let him lay a hand on me. No free samples. You don't know Pops Martin, and I do. Any girl who gives him what he wants can forget it."

"So, you're still the virgin bride?"

Her laugh was like enamel cracking. "Yeah, that's right. Come over here and see what you can do about that." She raised both arms invitingly, and the front of her nightie did another nose-dive.

"I'd like to, Genie," I said without moving. "I really would."

"Well, then?"

"One little thing bothers me. I can understand that you're disappointed at Pops' lack of enthusiasm for honeymoon calisthenics. But it still seems to me that marrying him was a pretty drastic step. What was keeping you from kissing off the dishpan and Pops Martin and just hitting the road?"

"These." She turned both thin arms elbows down, palms up. "Come over and have a close look," she said.

That intrigued me, and I did. At first, in the flat light, I couldn't see anything unusual about her arms, but then in the blue-white crook of her elbow I could make out a pale pattern of tracks like the faded reminders of aerial bombing.

One major vein on her left arm had that destroyed look they sometimes get when a needle has been stuck in them a couple of hundred times too many.

"See?" she said with a bittersweet smile.

"I get your point. And you think this place helps?"

She shrugged, and the rest of the top of her nightgown fell, covering the needle tracks on her arms. She took my hands and pulled me toward her. It would have taken a more determined man than I was just at that moment to have pulled away, so I sat down next to her legs. "I haven't used any since I came here over a year ago," she said, "and it's the first time I've been clean since I was fourteen years old. I don't know what you think of The Institute, but it's better than the gutter, and I've been there."

I believed her. Whatever other kind of fraud Hugo Fischer was, The Institute seemed to work for some. I wondered whether it was because of him or in spite of him.

"Tell me, Genie," I said, "did you..."

"I'm tired of telling," she complained, slipping down to a horizontal position and trying to pull me on top of her. She didn't have to try very hard to be honest, and I was just kissing my chastity goodbye when the intercom directly over my head cleared its throat and began to bark.

"Attention all residents and guests! Attention all residents and guests! Gather in the Horizon Room immediately! Immediately!" said a voice that sounded suspiciously like Hugo Fischer bellowing into a garbage can.

"Shit!" said Genie, snapping to a sitting position. Her eyes rambled around the room looking for another exit, but there was only the window.

Just then an obscure rumbling commenced as feet hit the floors and doors began to fly open. In the hallway outside the door, a babble of sleepy voices broke out, and somebody with a heavy foot thundered by hitting all the doors with a blunt instrument and crying: "Up, up, up! Let's move it! Now!"

"What are we going to do?" Genie whispered, suddenly turning from teenage seductress to trapped rat. She struggled into the rest of her nightgown and jumped out of bed.

"I think I'll just stay here," I said. "I've never been much for midnight frolics. Fischer probably just wants to find out if anyone is having any interesting dreams."

"You can't," she said. "They'll come through all the rooms to see if anyone's missing. When Hugo calls a meeting, everybody comes."

By then, the noise from the hallway had risen to a modest din, and the gazelle in clodhoppers bounded by again, dealt my door a mortal blow and bleated: "Out, out, *owwwwwt!*"

"Then I guess we'll have to go," I said. "You weren't wearing anything else when you came up here, were you?" Genie was nervously nibbling her thumb and looking sick. "No!" she wailed. "Christ, Pops is going to kill me for this."

"No, he won't," I said, trying to comfort her. After all, it was her honeymoon, and she'd already had two disappointments that night. "Tell me, who's sleeping on this floor?"

The panic began to drain from Genie's face. Maybe she figured I knew what I was doing. "Mostly guests," she said, "and maybe a couple of newcomers."

Outside in the hall, I could still hear a bit of scampering about, but it was dying down as the sleepyheads filtered downstairs.

"Just a second," I told Genie. Opening the door carefully, I stuck my head, out into the hall, making sure that no passerby could see into my room. Just my luck, Rachel Schute was just coming out into the hall knotting the sash of an apple-green dressing gown. Redheads ought to always wear green.

"Hello, Joe," she said, a bit startled to suddenly see me. There was something else in her expression.

"Hi, Rachel," I said. "Isn't this fun? What do you suppose the great man wants?"

"We'll find out when we get downstairs," she said, with reproof in her voice. "Are you ready to go down?" She paused and turned toward me as if waiting for me to join her.

"Uh, no—no," I said a bit hurriedly. "I've got a couple of —uh—things to do. You go right ahead. I'll be right there. Save me a seat."

Rachel looked puzzled, bit her lower lip and said: "All right, Joe. I'll see you downstairs. But don't be too long. Hugo likes people to be prompt."

"I'll bet," I said to her departing back. I was watching her about to disappear down the stairs when she looked back at me. I shut the door in a hurry.

Back inside my room, Genie was flitting here and there in her bridal nightie like a nubile moth. "Listen," I said. "I think everyone's gone down from this floor. I'll check again, and then we can creep down before Fischer sends his bloodhounds up to sniff us out. Where is your room?"

"On the next floor down," she said.

"Right," I said. "I'll go down the stairs first. If the way is clear, I'll whistle and head on downstairs to the big meeting. You make it to Pops' room and get something on."

"But what will I tell Pops? Remember, I was supposed to be in bed with him."

"Tell him anything," I suggested helpfully. "Tell him he didn't wake up when the first announcement came and that you rushed out of the room before he did. Tell him anything but the truth."

"Well, okay," she said doubtfully.

"Right," I said. "You ready?" She nodded, and I turned to open the door again.

"Joe?" she said, and I turned back to find her in my arms. She was like an armload of animated meringue, and I didn't fight very hard when she kissed me. Her lips tasted like perfumed orange Kool-Aid. "Thanks," she said, when she'd stopped molesting me, "for caring whether I get caught."

"It's nothing," I said, putting her feet back on the floor, "but we're both going to get caught if we don't get moving." A peek out of the door told me that the hall was deserted, and I moved out into it, whispering: "Follow me."

It was clear sailing to the head of the stairs. "You stay here, now," I said, "until I whistle. Then run like hell. If I start talking to someone in a loud voice, you'd better make it back to my room."

"Then what?" she asked, not looking as confident as she had a few moments before.

"God knows." I gave her hand a squeeze and started down the stairs. The next floor down was deserted. Giving the best whistle I could manage, I started blithely to turn toward the next flight only to come face to face with a breathless Rachel Schute.

"Joe," she said. "I forgot..."

Whatever she forgot was soon forgotten as her eyes caught sight of someone we both knew coming down the stairs behind me. Rachel's face froze in surprise that was about to turn to something else when she spun around and flew back down the stairs.

Genie was frozen, too, with one bare foot in the air, but

I dashed back and yanked her down to the next landing. Once her feet touched the floor again, I gave her a shove in the general direction of her room and then carried on down the stairs trying to whistle nonchalantly through a bone-dry throat.

12

WHEN I GOT DOWNSTAIRS, MOST OF THE MOB HAD filtered into the large drawing room that seemed to be the Horizon Room. I followed along, keeping close to the walls and playing the interested but detached observer. The last thing I wanted to do was draw attention to myself, which made it doubly unfortunate that I was just about the only one there who was fully dressed. My clothes aren't much at the best of times, but even after being dropped in the dirt by J. B. Carter, I stood out like Diamond Jim Brady at a slumber party.

When I got into the big—and now crowded—room, it hadn't changed much since that afternoon except that someone had spray-painted HUGO FUCK YOURSELF!!! on the expensive embossed wallpaper in a nasty shade of purple paint.

I began to get a glimmer why Fischer had asked us all to join him. And why that same charismatic figure was standing barefoot in a bright yellow terrycloth robe in front of a massive fireplace glaring at the assemblage. His birthmark seemed to be especially livid. Flanking him were Don

Moffitt, looking as though he wanted to maim somebody—anybody—and Pops Martin, who was trying to be tough but mostly looked sleepy and a bit bewildered. He was peering around the room anxiously. I spotted Rachel among the crowd, but she studiously refused to acknowledge that I existed.

There weren't enough chairs and couches, so most of us perched on window sills or just leaned against the walls. I was a leaner, myself. My watch told me it was after 2 a.m., and my head still throbbed where J.B. had sandbagged me. I noted that among those in the high priced seats were Mrs. J.B.—Tommy slumped beside her looking like a big baby in a set of woolly green pajamas—Rachel, Cousin Harold, Mrs. Harold and Dr. Carey. First among equals, you might say. Fischer's wife, Lenore, was sitting behind his right shoulder looking played out.

A half-moon-shaped area between Fischer and the front row was left vacant, and he stalked its periphery while security men in gray coveralls moved among the crowd, taking a head count. Finally, one of them sidled up to him and announced that all residents and guests were present or accounted for. Just then, out of the corner of my eye, I saw Genie tucked neatly in a far corner of the big room. She was swaddled to the chin in a very demure fuzzy blue kimono, and doing her best to be invisible. She wasn't looking anywhere near me, and that suited me fine. Just at that moment, Pops spotted her, too, and his face was a confusion of emotions. Before he could decide which of them to vent, however, Hugo put his big hands on his hips and began to speak.

"We're all here, friends," Fischer said, "so I suppose we can begin." A graveyard stillness fell over the room. Fischer surveyed us all for an uncomfortably long time, as if trying to extract a confession by sheer will power. The strain in the room was palpable, and I was thinking of confessing myself when Fischer broke the silence.

"Look about you, friends," he intoned, "and see the handiwork of one among us." He raked us with Gatling gun eyes, and we all dutifully inspected the graffiti as if we'd been looking at much else since we'd come into the room.

"Isn't it *beautiful*?" he cracked the word like a whip, pouring the maximum scorn on the scrawl and its anonymous author. "Isn't it witty? Doesn't it strike right at the heart of authority?"

Me, I didn't think it was so wonderful. I'd seen better in public toilets. I'd *written* better.

"Hank Willis!" The name rang out like a shot, and a depressed looking guy with a receding hairline and matching chin stopped studying his thumb and gave all his attention to Fischer. He didn't actually say: "Yes, Sir!" but he certainly began to look a lot more alert.

"Hank," said Hugo, in a benign tone with a hook in it, "why don't you read to us the work of the Phantom Scrawler?"

I'll give Willis some credit: He had the guts to shoot Fischer a "what the hell for?" look and keep his lip buttoned.

"Go right ahead," said Fischer with a flourish of his right hand. "We're all listening."

Willis opened his mouth. I'm not all that sure that he was going to obey Fischer, but Fischer didn't give him a chance.

"Oh, not from there, Hank," he said with deceptive bonhomie. "Come over here"—he pointed to the empty crescent before him—"where we can all see you and hear you."

Willis thought about that a lot, and looked around at the others as if to gather support. But a corridor to the place of honor was already opening for him. For a moment, I thought he wasn't going to take advantage of it. He stood, his eyes on Fischer's fleshy, flawed face, as if trying to read something that wasn't there. But Fischer's expression of benign impatience didn't change.

"Come on, Hank," he said. "We're all waiting."

Willis squared his puny shoulders and began to move through the crowded room. He didn't look at anyone in particular as he walked, but Susan Wallstrom—looking sleepily attractive in a soft-pink house coat—seemed to be trying to communicate some sort of support to him. If Willis received it, he wasn't letting on.

When he got to the dead center of Fischer's little no man's land, Willis stopped and once again looked into Hugo's eyes. His expression said: "All right, I know it's crazy, but I'm here." I wouldn't say it was exactly a duel; Fischer was too powerful for that. He could have blown Willis away without trying. But in a chicken shit way, it was a sort of rebellion, and I could tell that Fischer didn't like it. Not in front of the children.

Moffitt and Pops Martin didn't like it much either. They strained at invisible leads, as if ready to rip out Willis' throat on command. And they weren't the only ones. The look on the faces of the lads in gray was positively predatory. I wasn't sorry that it was Willis up there in the limelight instead of me.

The silence got on Pops' already taut nerves and he snapped: "All right, sucker, start reading!"

But Fischer reined him in with a small gesture of his hand. "Oh no, Pops, not yet. Hank looks a bit lonely standing there by himself, don't you think? Don't you think he could use some company?"

"Yeah!" said Don Moffitt, with more enthusiasm than was strictly necessary. He raked the assemblage with a jagged look. I noticed that his look went right over the heads of the folks in the two-dollar seats up front. Rachel didn't look worried. She was mesmerized, as if she were an anthropologist watching a cruel but fascinating ritual. But a lot of the company did. I imagined there was a certain amount of conscience-rummaging going on.

"What do you think, Hank?" Fischer asked, in a favorite-uncle tone of voice. "Could you use a little company?" Without waiting for an answer, he continued: "Like perhaps Vinnie Segundo?" His smile was alarming. "Come on up, Vinnie. Hank's lonely."

Vinnie, a dough-faced Italian boy in his early twenties with modishly long hair and slightly tinted gold-rimmed glasses, gulped audibly. "M-me, Hugo?" he said, after swallowing with difficulty. "Why me? I didn't..."

Whatever Vinnie didn't, didn't seem to matter very much as someone in the rear gave him a helpful shove, and he found himself being propelled up to Willis's side. There was a scattering of knowing smiles, and I got the feeling that perhaps Mr. Vincent Segundo wasn't a leading member of the community.

"And how about the young lovers?" Fischer shouted in a cheerleader fashion. "Shall we get them up here, too?"

"Yay!" cheered a bloodthirsty voice from the back, and Fischer gestured to a couple of his running dogs who left the room by a side door.

Things were getting lively now, and sleepy expressions had been replaced by emotions ranging from pity to anticipation to mild terror. But at least no one looked bored.

Fischer sure knew how to throw a party. I seemed forgotten for the moment, which didn't make me unhappy.

Willis, I'm sure, would have liked to be just as forgotten. Things had taken a turn for the worse for him in the last few minutes, and his face showed it. Things had begun to get out of hand. Willis recoiled from Vinnie as though he were carrying the Black Plague. It was a small space they were standing in, but Willis made the most of it. Vinnie just stood scratching his dandruff.

All eyes jumped to the side door as the gray wolves returned leading two grotesque creatures behind him. At first I thought it was a joke—a bad joke. Both were dressed in the black-and-white striped coveralls of cartoon convicts, and their heads hung forward. The head of the boy in front was shaved completely except for a one-inch swath from his forehead to the nape of his neck. The girl behind him had her fair hair tied up in dozens of ugly little clumps with faded ribbons and string. Then I recognized them as Lennie and Barbara, the runaways who had returned that afternoon during the wedding reception.

There was an involuntary sound from the crowd, half gasp, half sigh, as they caught sight of the couple. Rachel looked as though she were going to cry, but then bit her lip and forced her face back to a neutral expression. I glanced at Susan Wallstrom and was surprised to find her face completely devoid of any emotion. She was totally caught up in the spectacle. Behind the three chief inquisitors, Lenore Fischer's face was like a death mask, and her eyes weren't on the scene in the room.

Willis's expression did a few gyrations as the security men led the boy and girl through the crowd. This was turning into a freak show, but he couldn't think of any way to get out of it.

"Welcome," said Fischer sardonically, but neither of the newcomers could manage to look up at him. "Now, let's see," he said mischievously, rubbing his stubbly chin, "who else?"

"Bob Fuller!" someone shouted, and I followed the mob's eyes to one corner where an apparition slumped against the wall, apparently asleep. He was about thirty and fattish, with skin the color of putty and thinning black hair combed straight back from a mole-like face. He was wearing an ancient, rusty black, ankle-length raincoat, which looked as though it had been slept in.

"Wha—?" Fuller muttered, when someone poked him, but eventually he sleep-stumbled up to join the growing circus at the front of the room. If Willis had shied away from Vinnie Segundo, at the advent of this newcomer he began to climb the walls.

Fischer called for another couple of reluctant volunteers —a thin, bitter-faced girl with a build of a lady high jumper, and a handsome black boy with the languid air of a Zulu prince—and the company of pariahs seemed to be complete.

Fischer looked around the room with jovial menace. "I think that'll do, don't you?" he asked us. "Or would somebody else like to join this little band?"

Somehow none of us did. Clasping his hands like the bride's father at a Polish wedding, Fischer beamed at Willis and said: "Perhaps now, Hank, you'll be kind enough to read what is written on the wall."

From the expression on his face, there was nothing Willis would have liked to do less, except perhaps swallow his tongue. But he pivoted back toward the graffiti and recited in a voice as flat as the Plains of Abraham: "Hugo fuck yourself."

"Excuse me, Hank," Fischer said with mock politeness.

"I didn't quite catch that. Do you think you could read it just one more time?"

There may have been someone in that room—besides the Mad Dog and his pups—who was enjoying this spectacle, but it wasn't Willis. He toughed it out, though, and his face was blank as he repeated: "Hugo fuck yourself."

"Thank you," said Fischer. "Did everybody hear that?"

"I didn't!" called out a tall wise guy near the side door. "Well," rasped out Fischer, "for you and the other illiterates, it says: Hugo fuck yourself."

The tall guy shrank until he could have fitted into Fischer's vest pocket, and most everybody else looked suitably scandalized. Fischer had spoken the words with a Shakespearean roundness that Hank Willis hadn't quite been able to muster.

"Hugo fuck yourself," Fischer said again, but this time it was spoken softly, as if to himself. Now he was a ruminative Zeus wondering who'd had the hubris to piss on his leg. He repeated it, softly yet ringingly, and then raised his great, flawed head to take in all of us. "What can that mean?" he asked with his hands raised imploringly. Now he was Moses having a private chat with God. Fischer sure could run the gamut. Any minute, now, I expected him to speak in tongues or do the splits.

Instead, he zeroed in on Willis again. "Hank," he said, "you're a writer, a literary man. Can you tell us what it means?" When Willis didn't respond immediately, Fischer darkened as though he was going to rain all over him and demanded: "What does it mean!"

I didn't know about the rest of them, but I was getting a bit bored with this scenario. Not to mention, Fischer may have been the greatest performer since John Wilkes Booth, but not at nearly three in the morning.

"I think, Mr. Fischer," I said in the kind of voice you use on a suspect in a police line-up, "it's a pun, what you'd call a play on words."

I certainly had everybody's attention, even Hugo Fischer's. He pointed his heavy brow toward me in surprise: "Is it, Mr. Goodey? Is it now? A pun, you say. I thought you were a detective, not a semanticist."

Hank Willis looked relieved to be out of the spotlight. Rachel was shaking her head at me in warning, and Moffit and Pops Martin licked their lips and looked hungry.

I didn't say anything, so Fischer went on: "Perhaps," he said, playing to the cheap seats, "we could prevail on Mr. Goodey, our visiting linguistics expert, to expound on the literary merits of the work of the midnight scrawler. Do you think you could do that, Mr. Goodey?"

I really had the group's attention now. There was something tribal in their faces, something mystical and savage that made me glad that I was just a stranger passing through. "I could, I suppose, Mr. Fischer," I said, "but not just now. I'm tired and I'm going to bed."

Without bothering to read any faces, I turned and walked from the big drawing room. There was a security guard on either side of the doorway, but neither made a move. They stood like toy soldiers with open mouths.

Behind me, all was silent for a long, long moment. Then there was an explosion of sound, an angry clamoring punctuated by what I'd have sworn was the barking of dogs. I half expected to hear the heavy thump of running steps coming after me, but I was still alone when I got to the stairs. The racket from the Horizon Room seemed to grow even louder, but then as I climbed it faded, until from the top floor I could hear only a dull roar like rushing water.

When I closed the door to my room even that died

down. At that late hour, the under-butler's hard, thin bed was as welcoming as a bower of roses. The pungent shadow of Genie's perfume lingered in the sheets, and the last thing I remembered before I fell asleep was the rustle of her translucent negligee.

13

SOMETIME DURING THE MORNING I DIMLY PERCEIVED the intercom announcing that breakfast was being served, and I considered the possibility. But just then the sandman in the guise of J. B. Carter let me have it behind the left ear, and the next thing I knew my wristwatch said it was nearly noon.

When my feet hit the floor, I became aware of two things: my aching head and a flash of white on the floor just inside the door. It turned out to be a folded piece of paper. When I could get my eyes into focus, I read: "If you want to know who killed Katie, it was Rudolph Verrein. A friend."

I had to treat this with suspicion. As far as I knew, I didn't have a friend at The Institute. Especially after being caught on the stairs between Genie and Rachel the night before. But it certainly was interesting, whoever Rudolph Verrein might turn out to be.

The intercom above my bed made vague noises, but before it could decide what to say, I stepped up on the bed, wrenched the damned thing off the wall and lobbed it into the wastepaper basket. Then it occurred to me that it might have been about to inform me that the building was on fire. The dead speaker looked at me accusingly from the basket.

When I took my towel and shaving kit out into the communal bathroom, it was empty except for Roscoe Matson in bright red shorts glowering at his image in the mirror as if trying to hypnotize it.

"Hi," I said, because I'm a very friendly guy.

He started to return my greeting but then said something that sounded like *mmmph* and turned to glare at me. "Hey, man," he said belligerently, "I'm not talking to you."

"How's that?"

"You know. That session last night. You fucked it up for fair with your wise mouth."

"Sorry," I said with as much sincerity as I could manage. "I'm a new boy around here, you know. Don't know all the ropes."

"You sure don't," he said, "and if you don't wise up somewhat, you may not live to be an old boy." With that, he gathered up his shaving gear and headed for the door.

"Hey, Roscoe," I said, before he could quite make it. He stopped, looked back at me and grunted: "Hummmph?"

"I know we're not buddies anymore," I said, "but do you think you could tell me who Rudolph Verrein is?"

"Rudy Verrein is a son of a bitch," said Matson.

"Be that as it may," I said. "Do you have any idea where I could find him?"

"I hope he's in hell," said Matson, "and I wouldn't mind a whole lot if you were there with him." With that, he flipped his towel over his shoulder and stalked out.

Feeling a bit cleaner but just as friendless as ever, I tramped down the stairs to find out what wonders that Sunday at The Institute would bring. The downstairs hall was nearly empty, and I saw nobody I knew.

Just then the aroma of food wafting from the dining room hit me, and I remembered that I'd slept through breakfast. As I was walking in that direction, something caught my eye in a room off to one side of the hall. It was Hank Willis behind a bar, pouring a big pot of steaming water into a coffee urn. I considered ignoring my stomach and going in to have a chat, but then I became aware of his face. It was the face of a man studying the fine print of his soul and not liking what he read. Even a man more famous for his insensitivity than I wouldn't have barged in on Willis's communion with Inner Truth. At least not while he had a pot of boiling water in his hand.

So I tiptoed on past to the dining room. I didn't get a standing ovation from the lunch-eaters, but then nobody threw a knife at me, either. Spotting an empty chair beside Susan Wallstrom, I slipped into it before anyone could start forming a lynch mob.

"Hello, Susan," I said.

She didn't look too happy to see me, but good manners prevented her from spitting in my eye. She said hello nicely enough, but didn't seem eager to go much further.

I helped myself to whatever looked edible and asked her: "What time did that clambake end last night?"

That may not have been the right question. "We all went to bed about four-thirty," she said, a bit sniffily. "I hope you got enough sleep."

"Nearly," I said. "But that's really not why I left early. I just didn't care much for Fischer's idea of midnight frolics. Did you? You didn't look too happy to me last night."

I began to notice that some of our tablemates had stopped grazing and were tuning in on our conversation. So did Susan, and the idea didn't delight her.

"There are a lot of things, Mr. Goodey," she said, "that you don't understand about The Institute."

I'd heard that refrain before, but rather than explore it just then I decided to change the subject.

"That's becoming more obvious by the minute," I said. "But I'm trying to learn. And there's something else I'd like to learn: Who is Rudolph Verrein?"

From her expression, Susan didn't like my new topic much better than the old one, but she answered: "He's a portrait painter and a former friend of The Institute. He lives in Las Palomas."

"Why former?" I asked, but lowered my voice to a level that I hoped only Susan could hear. Privacy was probably a sin at The Institute, but I liked it. "What did he do—accuse Fischer of being human?"

Another wrong thing to say. Susan wrinkled her pretty Scandinavian nose in distaste and said: "I don't know why Rudy is no longer a friend of The Institute. Why don't you ask Hugo?"

"I'll do better than that," I said, spearing a last string bean and standing up. "I'll ask Rudolph Verrein. See you later."

Susan was too busy chasing diced carrots around on her plate to answer, so I turned away and headed for the dining room door. On the way, I looked around for familiar faces. Fischer was nowhere to be seen, but Rachel and Jim Carey were eating forehead to forehead in one corner and talking something over intently. The honeymoon couple sat alone at another small table. Pops still looked a bit sulky, but from her expression Genie had things under control again. She raised an eyebrow that I pretended not to see. At that moment, Pops swiveled in my direction not looking very friendly, but she said something, and he turned back.

I was just about at the door when a large, strong hand grabbed my arm and helped me turn back around. A glowering face under a narrow forehead that belonged to a caveman stared down at me with hostility. I recalled seeing him at the table helping beans onto his fork with an outsized thumb. "You were asking about Rudy Verrein?" he asked.

"Yes," I said, "but I wasn't asking you." He gave my arm a little shake of impatience that I felt down to my last vertebra. "But if you'd like to answer," I said, "I'd certainly be grateful."

That didn't seem to placate him much, but he threw my arm down as if he had no further use for it.

"I'll tell you who Rudy Verrein is," he said. "He's a faggot bastard who got thrown out of here for going around always trying to fuck our girls."

I didn't bother asking him to clear up this apparent contradiction, just thanked him very much and turned to continue toward the door, hoping not to be retrieved again.

"You tell Rudy to stay the hell away from here," he shouted at my retreating back, "or he'll get his scrawny neck broken. Tell him Jerry Wildenradt said so."

I couldn't help turning back at the doorway, and discovered every eye in the place turned toward our little scene. I tried to think of a comeback that wouldn't get my neck broken in five places. "How do you spell that?" I asked him.

"W-i-l..."he started, but then something told Wildenradt I just might be having him on, and a carmine flush began to rise in his fleshy chops.

I took several rapid steps down the hall and was soon in the marble foyer on the way out of the mansion when something caught my eye. It was a vast oil portrait of Hugo Fischer high up on the wall over the front door. I didn't have to guess that Verrein had done it. The pose was pugnaciously Churchillian, the technique bold with a rough, cobbled surface that looked as though it had been achieved with a blunt weapon. This wasn't a school of painting I usually liked, but in this portrait Verrein had made Fischer several sizes larger than life and had infused the birthmark with something noble, even tragic.

In all, it was a majestic portrait that I could imagine Fischer spending a lot of time gazing at. I wouldn't have gone out of my way to make an enemy of someone who could have made me look like that. But then, I wasn't Fischer, and I hadn't met Verrein yet, either.

The security guards at the barrier dented ice pick looks on the front of the Morris, but grudgingly let me pass. On Highway 1 in downtown Las Palomas—a general store, a post office and a Shell station—the pump jockey, a vest-pocket hipster in mirror shades, told me how to get to Rudolph Verrein's, adding: "Some pretty freaky things go on down there, man."

I thanked him for the warning and drove down the highway until my eagle eye caught an inconspicuous break in the hedge on the seaward side and a small bronze plaque with the initials R.V. I wheeled into the break and drove down an access road similar to the one leading to The Institute's mansion. But there were no security guards, and at the end of it lay not a gingerbread extravaganza but an architect's dream house in redwood and plate glass that lay against the landscape as if it had grown there.

I stopped the Morris next to a Lotus Elan in a little clearing under some eucalyptus trees and had started to open the door when my eye was caught by something moving toward me through the leaf-strained sunshine at a menacing gait. I blinked and it had disappeared. Then it was there again, a piebald Great Dane making slightly better than ramming speed in my direction. I had second thoughts about getting out of the car and rolled up the window.

The big dog came to a splay-footed stop with his long tongue lolling wetly and was probably wondering whether to eat the whole car just to get a taste of me when we both heard a commanding voice call: "King!"

A check of my dog tag told me it wasn't me. King turned around in a single movement and bounded toward a tall man coming to the car from the house.

He was dressed for riding in a musical-comedy sort of way. Impeccably tailored jodhpurs rose from polo boots as if they were one unit he'd been ladled into, and the whole effect was topped off with a silk paisley-printed scarf that seemed to be holding his head on. His face suggested a minor Russian prince who'd been born under a sun lamp. The swollen veins in his fine Romanov nose hinted loudly of too many bottles of twelve-year-old Scotch, and the tinkle of ice cubes from the glass in his left hand reinforced the idea. His right hand was taken up by a riding crop that had never bothered a horse.

"Don't worry, old boy," he said, leaning down and peering at me. "King wouldn't hurt a fly. I keep him mostly for effect." Behind him, King sat down and besieged a flea behind his left ear as if to prove that he, too, had human foibles. "I'm Rudolph Verrein. Can I help you?"

Rather than hold the interview in my car, which King could have carried away and buried, anyway, I slipped out of the Morris, keeping Verrein between me and the dog.

"My name's Joe Goodey, Mr. Verrein," I said, giving him a peek at my credentials. "I'm over at The Institute trying to find out who killed Katie Pierce."

The change in his expression was instantaneous. No

longer was it languid. His eyes took on a hard, Baltic glitter, and if he'd had a mustache it would have bristled. "Ah!" he barked. "They told you I did it, did they? Who was it? Don Moffitt? Pops? Perhaps Jim Carey? They're all charlatans and liars!"

"No, no...wait," I said soothingly. "It's not like that at all. It just occurred to me that perhaps you could tell me some things about The Institute and Katie Pierce that I couldn't learn over there."

"Ah, Katya," he said softly, and the Cossack bluster was gone. His mobile features were a study in Slavic tenderness. "Poor, poor Katya." I half expected him to whip out a gypsy violin. But instead he gulped his drink, and bisected an ice cube with large, white teeth. "Come," said Verrein with a flourish, "I will do what I can to help you. I can tell you a lot." He spun and stalked toward his house.

The interior of Verrein's house was as spectacular as the outside. It gave the impression of having been built around a natural outcropping of rough granite, laced with a spectacular array of exotic house plants and set in a frame of oiled teak, stripped pine and the ubiquitous plate glass. A cunningly contrived indoor waterfall trickled down a pile of expensive rocks to a free-form swimming pool set in a grassy terrace on the seaward side of the house. I put a finger in the waterfall; it was blood warm.

I followed Verrein into a large airy studio like a glass box on the north side of the house. It was Spartan in the extreme, containing only a paint-splattered easel, a few Eames chairs and a naked sixteen-year-old girl sitting on a padded stool reading a comic book and popping black grapes into a softly carnivorous little mouth. Her smoky eyes registered my presence but showed no signs of modesty or alarm.

"Rudy, darling," she said, stretching showily, "haven't we done enough today? I promised to go surfing."

As I passed his easel, I noticed that he had half-finished an idealized head and shoulders portrait in which the girl looked like a hip Scarlett O'Hara. Presumably, she was naked because Verrein was trying to portray the inner woman.

"Of course," said Verrein, with the deference money and beauty attract. "You run along, and I'll see you at the same time tomorrow morning." She reached a hand down beside the stool, and as if by sleight of hand she was suddenly dressed in a pair of skin-tight Levis and a midnight-blue velvet top. She must have saved a lot on underwear bills.

"Kelly De Freese—Joe Goodey," said Verrein by way of introduction. "Kelly is making her debut in Carmel this summer," he added. "And I am immortalizing her beauty. Kelly, Joe is a detective from San Francisco. He's come down here to solve a murder."

She murmured: "Oh," as if he'd said that I liked blueberry pie and wore size nine and a half D shoes. "Hello. See you." And she was gone.

"Does Mama know that little Kelly sits for her portrait in the buff, Mr. Verrein?" I asked.

"Call me Rudy," he said. "Of course. It's the only way I paint women. That's Violet De Freese up there." I followed his finger to a large portrait of a Rubens-esque blonde lying back on a brass bed showing a lot of skin. I could see where Kelly got the eyes and a few other things.

"Sit down," he said, indicating one of the chairs. "Now, how can I help you?"

"As I understand it," I said, "you were very close to Hugo Fischer and The Institute in the months before Katie

Pierce died, but that you've fallen out with them. Would you mind telling me why?"

"What did they say?" he demanded with a slightly cunning expression on his narrow face.

"Jerry Wildenradt said it was because you spent most of your time chasing girls at The Institute," I said. "He added that he'd like to break your neck."

To my surprise, Verrein responded not angrily but softly. "Ah, Jerry," he said. "We were good friends once."

"He didn't seem to think so," I said. "What's your version?"

"I'd have to go quite a way back to explain that," he said, gesturing expressively with a hand that shot out in a flourish and ended up drumming on his brown forehead with three fingers. He looked pensive.

"Tell me," I said and put on my listening-attentively face.

Leaving out a certain amount of Slavic embroidery, Verrein's story was that when The Institute had come to squat in J. B. Carter's mansion, he hadn't seen much charm in having the neighborhood overrun with drug addicts, criminals and other undesirables. He'd signed petitions, chipped in for lawyer's fees and rained protests on the head of Sheriff Dominguez. All to no avail. Fischer was on perfectly sound legal ground, and all the antis could do were seethe and hope that one of the dopers would do something to get The Institute thrown out by the authorities.

But then came a personal invitation from Hugo Fischer urging Verrein and other influential neighbors to visit The Institute for an open house. Verrein at first rejected the idea, but then decided to go along—partly out of curiosity.

But—surprise, surprise—Hugo Fischer turned on his

massive charm, the residents of The Institute couldn't have been more appealing and winsome, and Rudolph Verrein was converted almost instantly from an enemy to a new supporter of The Institute.

"The most impressive thing," said Verrein, "was that Hugo and the others seemed to be living such clean, worthwhile lives without the compromises which seem to be necessary to the rest of us." A fluid gesture included Mama De Freese's portrait on the wall and the unfinished one of Kelly. "I'm not kidding myself that this is what an artist should be doing."

Once clasped to Hugo's bosom and initiated in the mysteries of The Institute, Verrein became a very tight friend indeed. "I painted that portrait of Hugo," he said, "which is the best thing I've ever done, became chairman of the sponsors group and spent more time over there than I did here. I think it was the happiest time of my life." He looked wistful.

"So what happened?" I asked.

"To this day, I really don't know," he said, and his bewilderment seemed genuine. "Things were going so well. I was happy, and I had great plans for a really splendid art exhibition that would have brought money and good publicity to The Institute. But then, suddenly, overnight, I was frozen out. I was an enemy. People I'd come to love like brothers and sisters spat when my name was mentioned." The memory brought pain with it.

"When was this?"

"Early last December," he said. "The art exhibition was to have been at Christmas time. But of course there was none." He looked like a kid who'd been crossed off Santa's list.

"But you don't know why you were frozen out?" I

persisted. "It couldn't have been over girls at The Institute as Wildenradt said?"

He thought about that for a long time, massaging his lean jaw lovingly. "No, I honestly don't think so. I'll be honest with you, I like girls, young girls." He peeked at me to see how I was taking this revelation. "And there is no shortage of friendly young girls at The Institute."

"Could the big freeze have had anything to do with Katie?" I asked, not really hoping for much from the question.

He started to answer no automatically, but then paused. "I don't think so," he said, "but..."

"But what?"

"Well, something a bit strange did happen just before... before I wasn't welcome at The Institute any more. I didn't really know Katie very well. When she'd first come to live there her mind was so confused that it was hard to communicate with her at all. But," Verrein went on, "the longer Katie stayed at The Institute, the better she seemed to get, and I began to notice that this was no ordinary girl. There was something very special about her. You could call it soul, if you like. And as autumn came on I got to know her and to like her very much. You know, Katie was a very good singer. And she played guitar, too. I can still remember her sitting on the terrace, playing and singing 'Sad-Eyed Lady of the Lowlands.' You know, the Bob Dylan song."

I nodded appreciatively just to keep him going. He closed his eyes soulfully and swayed a little, recapturing the scene. I could almost see it myself.

"Katie and I became quite close," he said. "I liked her, and I'm pretty sure she thought of me as something more than a friend."

There must have been some doubt in my expression

because Verrein drew himself up like a goosed librarian and insisted: "I know what you're thinking, but you're wrong. Katie wasn't ready for that yet. I'm not saying that one day... but I swear to you, at that time there was nothing between us but affection, purely affection."

"I believe you," I said, as sincerely as possible, not adding that there were thousands who wouldn't. "But you were saying that something strange happened, possibly because you were...close to Katie."

He let the little hesitation pass. "Yes, it was very odd," he said. "I began to notice that some of the old-timers had begun to give me hard looks when I came around the mansion. These were mostly former drug addicts. I've never found it easy to understand the drug addict's mentality, anyway. To me, The Institute had gone a long way past the stage of just drying them out and keeping them away from the needle."

"You began to sense that someone wasn't too happy with your behavior," I said.

"To put it mildly," he said. "I began to encounter real hostility at The Institute. Even Tommy Carter seemed to be unfriendly. At first, I shrugged it off, but then, late in November, Don Moffitt got in on the act."

"He was trying to protect Katie's chastity, too?" I asked.

"I don't know," Verrein said. "I've never liked Moffitt. I think he's a thug. And when he started to lean on me about Katie, I'm afraid I overreacted. I told him to stay the hell out of my business."

"And then the iron curtain came down," I said.

"No," Verrein said. "Not exactly. You see," he said with a self-mocking laugh, "I was convinced that I was a pretty important person around The Institute, and that I could handle professional hard nuts like Moffitt."

"But you were wrong," I prompted.

"I guess so," he said. "Nothing happened at first, except I kept catching a lot of hostility from the dope fiends. Moffitt pretended I didn't exist, but I didn't mind that. But then one day early in December I was sitting in the Horizon Room with some friends when Hugo came wandering in and said casually: 'Oh, Rudy, about that art exhibition thing you've been planning; it's off.' I didn't understand at first, but then it finally got through to me that something on which I'd spent months of work and string-pulling was suddenly, arbitrarily canceled."

"That was tough," I said.

"It was worse than that," he said. "To me it was a tragedy, and I tried to get Hugo to give me a reason. But he wouldn't. He just said something about The Institute having more important things to do than mess around with such artsy-craftsy bullshit, and left me standing there. I went home feeling sick about it. And the next day when I tried to drive to the mansion, the security men wouldn't let me through. They said my name wasn't on the list of approved guests."

"Fischer disappeared you, eh?" I asked, not too surprised to hear it.

"I just don't know," said Verrein gloomily. "I don't want to believe it, but..." He made a palms-up gesture of helplessness and dismay. "I tried to call Hugo; I wrote him letters, but nothing happened. I was a nonperson as far as The Institute was concerned. But do you know what I think?" He looked at me intensely.

"No, what?"

"I don't think it was Hugo at all. Oh, he made the decision, all right, but I'm sure that some of those mental cripples around Hugo poisoned him against me. I know it! But what can I do?" He slumped in his chair, the pugnacity going out of him.

"And you never saw Katie again." I asked. But he surprised me.

"Yes," he said. "Just once. One night about the middle of December—it was raining, I remember, a filthy night—I heard a knocking at the back door, and it was Katie. She'd walked all the way from the mansion, and she was soaking."

He paused, as if reliving the experience, then started again. "I brought her in, got her a towel and one of my robes, and we sat in front of the fire while her clothes dried. She said she'd just come over to see me, to have a chat, but there was something more than that. Something wrong. She wasn't the same Katie. I almost suspected..."

"That she'd gone back on pills?"

He didn't like the idea, but he said: "Yes. But even if that were true, there was something else. I could have sworn that Katie was afraid of something—really afraid. I tried to find out what, but she wouldn't talk about it. She started to, I think, several times, but then she would stop. She took my guitar down from the wall and sang some songs. You should have seen her, her hair still a bit wet and steaming from the heat of the fire, sitting there in my robe in the firelight, strumming the guitar and singing softly. It was..." He was lost in the image, and then the shadow of something unpleasant passed over his long features.

He broke out of his troubled reverie. "I couldn't help it," he said. "She was so beautiful. I reached out to touch her, and suddenly she jumped up from the hearth, screaming like a madwoman. Believe me, I didn't mean...I only...she frightened the life out of me. Before I could do anything to calm her, she pulled on her damp clothes and ran into the night. I never saw her again—alive—after that night."

He looked up at me, and we both sat in silence for a moment.

"Did you tell this to the police or to the Brazewell operatives?" I asked finally.

He shook his head. "No one," he said. "It was a very personal experience, and there didn't seem to be any point. It couldn't bring Katie back to life."

I agreed with him there. I seemed to have gotten about as much out of Rudolph Verrein as I was going to for the moment, so I stood up to leave him alone with his memories. He didn't say anything, just followed me out to the Morris and watched me climb in. King stood in the background looking like a dog that had just missed a good meal.

"One thing," I said. "When did you get that brute?"

"Last December," he said. "Just after I...left The Institute."

"You didn't think Fischer would send his lads over here to harass you, do you?"

Verrein pondered that one for a moment, then said: "No, I don't think Hugo would. But I'm not so sure of some of the others. There are some pretty desperate characters over there, you know, and some of them are not fond of me."

"You've got a point there," I said. "So long." But then I thought of something. "Is there any message you want me to give Fischer for you?"

His face brightened. "Yes," he said. "You can tell him that I...that I...ah, to hell with it." He turned around and started walking toward the house like a man going someplace to have a drink.

I nodded goodbye to King and headed for The Institute.

14

A GRAY-CLAD SECURITY MAN STRADDLED THE LONG, winding driveway down to the mansion and showed me his outstretched palm. I'd seen cleaner. His partner lounged near the lowered wooden barrier looking mean. It sure was good to be back home.

I waved cheerily, expecting the one playing traffic cop to jump aside and tug his forelock. He didn't. I had to abuse the Morris's brakes to avoid ruining the crease in his coveralls. Stiffly he walked around to the driver's window and looked at me blankly. "Goodey," I said as if talking to a half-wit. "Jonah Webster Goodey. Of San Francisco. California."

He'd have made a hell of a poker player. Without a flicker of recognition, he consulted his clipboard and told me: "I'm sorry, Mr. Goodey, you're not on the list of approved guests. I can't let you in." He gave me a flash of the guest list, and sure as hell, no Joe Goodey. Could it be? Had I become an official unperson at The Institute during my visit to Rudy Verrein? That possibility became more probable when I noticed sitting by the side of the driveway a suitcase that could have been mine. Fischer had made his move.

"That's the way it is, eh?" I said, giving him the smile of a good loser.

"That's the way it is," he said. "You can turn your car around just over there to the right." He picked my suitcase up and put it in the back of the car.

"Right," I said, tramping the accelerator to the floorboards and gunning the Morris directly at the wooden barrier. It didn't disintegrate the way they do in the movies, but it sure swiveled out of my way in a hurry, laying low the other guard, whose scowl had turned to a terrified grimace. Through the rearview mirror I got a satisfying glimpse of chaos in my wake.

I skidded to a halt in the parking lot at the side of the mansion and discovered that The Institute had other guests. Two squad cars from the Monterey County Sheriff's Department and an ambulance. A young deputy was leaning against one of the cars practicing his squint.

"What's happening?" I asked.

"That depends on who you are," he said.

I gave him a look at my I.D., adding: "Lieutenant Grenby knows I'm here." He read the card, moving his lips slightly, and then thought about it for a while.

Finally he said: "They're bringing some old dude up from the rocks." He gestured vaguely in the direction of the sheer rocks up above the mansion.

By the time I got near the top of the cliff, I was puffing and blowing like a gut-busted concertina and swimming in sweat. A black haze of exhaustion had settled over my eyes, and I made a vow to get in shape.

When I could see again, I got a good grip on the stitch in my side and continued along the cliff face with the sea on my left. I didn't get far before I was met by a grim little procession.

Leading it was Lieutenant Michael Grenby looking somber and efficient. Behind him was an anonymous man in his shirtsleeves carrying a medical bag and walking as if he were on a tightrope, although the edge of the cliff was a good ten feet away. Following them, a sheriff's deputy and two ambulance attendants in dirty hospital whites shouldered a body bag that looked to be half empty. Bringing up the rear was Hugo Fischer with Emma Carter leaning on his substantial shoulder. She wasn't crying, but her head lay against his collar bone at a peculiar angle as if her neck were broken. I didn't have to guess who was in the bag.

Grenby's eyes took me in without much joy. "I'll see you down at the house," he told me softly as he walked past. The man with the medical bag nodded politely, but the three bearers didn't even see me. All they wanted to do was get rid of their load. Mrs. Carter's blue-veined eyelids were tightly closed as she passed, but Fischer was all eyes. He didn't say anything, but his look said he had marked me up for later slaughter.

I watched the cortege out of sight around a bend and then proceeded along the path they'd just covered. In less than fifty yards, I was back just outside J. B. Carter's cave hideaway, where two more sheriff's men, wet to the armpits, were struggling to pack up a portable block and tackle and a thick reel of steel cable. With his back to me, a little man wearing sergeant's stripes and built-up shoes was watching their struggles but resisting the urge to jump in and help.

There was something familiar yet alien about the back of his head. The familiar part was his ears, low slung and slightly crimped as if recoiling from something they didn't want to hear. I knew those ears, but they didn't belong on that head. Then he said: "I think we're winning, boys," in a high, nasal voice, and I knew.

"You're doing a great job, Harry," I said, "but why aren't these lads giving you a hand?"

Harry Shearer turned around in a single graceful motion, and I suddenly knew why it had taken so long to recognize him. Since I'd seen him about a year and a half before, he'd acquired a head of thick, semi-wavy auburn hair that lay on his round little head like moss on a cannon ball. The last time I'd seen him he'd been trying to make six greasy strands cover about half an acre of highly polished scalp. I'd have to ask him how he did it, when I got up the nerve.

"Goodey," he said flatly. He showed about as much surprise as a chorus girl on her seventh honeymoon. "Grenby said you were hanging around, but I heard they gave you the boot." His eyes went to mine, and I started looking anywhere but at his hairline.

"Nah," I said. "They love me here." His snort said he'd have to see it in writing. "What's the scam?" Harry hesitated, so I said: "You may as well play know-it-all or Grenby will. He and I are like this." I held my two index fingers up and as far apart as my arms could get them.

"I believe it," Harry said. "How much do you know?"

"You just brought old man Carter up from the base of the cliff in something less than perfect condition," I said. "He didn't tell you how he got there."

"Wonderful, Joe," Harry said. "You know, you ought to be a detective."

"There's no money in it," I said. "What did he look like?"

"Not his best," Harry said. "Those rocks down there can play hell with the complexion."

"Did the coroner come to any instant conclusions?"

"Some," Harry said. Then he hesitated.

"Come on, Harry," I said wearily. "Grenby will tell me, and I'll see the coroner's report. Save me some time. I'm double-parked."

"All right," he said. "His best guess at this point is that death was fairly simultaneous with the old man's arrival at the rocks down there. The usual massive fractures, contusions, hemorrhaging, that sort of thing."

"It sounds like a carbon copy of the Pierce girl's injuries," I said.

"Close," Harry agreed, "but with one difference, Joe. According to the coroner, not all of Carter's injuries were sustained at the bottom. He suspects that he knows what put Carter there."

"And what would that be?"

"A fairly sharp blow across the superciliary arch. That's the lower forehead to you. Not hard enough to kill him, but with plenty of force to stun him or even put him out completely."

"And over?" I asked.

Shearer shrugged. "It sure didn't happen on the way down."

"Did the man happen to say how long Carter had been dead?"

"Not to the minute, but he brackets it between ten and fourteen hours. Isn't science wonderful?"

"Yeah, dazzling," I said. "You got any idea of who or what hit him? I mean, just a rough idea. Don't strain your mush."

He looked at me with wonder tinged with disgust. "Christ, Goodey, you're worse than Grenby, and I don't even work for you. No, I don't know what hit him, who was holding it or what sort of grip he was using. But I will, and if you read the newspapers, you will, too. What do you care, anyway? I thought the Pierce high dive was your meal ticket."

"It is," I said. "But I've got a bit of spare time on my hands, and I thought I might give you a hand. You know, in an amateur sort of way. Mind if I have a look around?" I gestured vaguely in the direction of the late J.B.'s cave hideaway.

"I sure as hell do," said Harry. "You take one step, and we're going to reenact the crime using you as a stand-in. Once I'm finished up here, you can nose around all you want. Until then, you keep away. Now, would you rather walk back to the mansion or take a short cut? Boys..." he said to his two bird dogs who had finished with the lifting tackle and were standing eyeing me coldly.

"That's okay, Harry," I said, backing off. "I'll walk. I need the exercise."

When I got back down to the mansion, Fischer was waiting for me on what in a less impressive house would have been called the front porch. He was backed by Moffitt and a couple of other thugs, and he didn't look happy. Grenby stood off to one side, leaning on a fluted pillar and trying to look detached yet in charge of things at the same time. He wasn't succeeding.

"You!" intoned Fischer, pointing a majestic finger at me as if it were about to flash lightning. "Get out! If you're not off my property in five minutes, you'll wish you'd never been born." He had apparently heard about the gate-crashing incident.

"I'm sorry, Mr. Fischer," I said, "I'd love to, but I can't. Not just yet."

"Can't!" Fischer shot the word at my head as if it were a bullet.

"I've got a job to do here," I said, trying to sound reasonable. "I can't do it if you throw me out."

Fischer's expression of Olympian disdain said he wasn't about to waste any more of his golden time on me. He was going to scrape me off his shoe like so much dog shit. "Don't," he said, and Moffitt and a couple of light-heavies took a step toward me.

I took a step backward and said: "Besides, I don't think Lieutenant Grenby can afford to lose his best suspect."

That stopped the mayhem squad cold, and even Fischer lost a little of his regal detachment. Grenby decided to let the pillar stand on its own and edged forward slightly. "What do you mean, Goodey?"

"I mean that it's very likely that I was the last person to talk to Carter before he was killed. Or the next to last, if you don't think I killed him."

"This is not something to joke about," Grenby said angrily. "An old man is dead."

"I'm not joking, Grenby," I said. "I spent quite a little time with Carter at around one o'clock this morning. If your coroner knows what he's doing, that was just before J.B. went over the cliff."

I snuck a look at Fischer's face, and something told me that I wasn't telling him anything new. I didn't think there was much that went on at The Institute that escaped his notice.

"What were you doing up there with Mr. Carter at that hour?" Grenby wanted to know.

"Oh, discussing this and that," I said. "Mostly who killed Katie Pierce."

That got a reaction, all right. Moffitt and his braves

snarled on cue, and Fischer started to puff up like a Christmas gobbler.

I appealed to Grenby: "Are you going to let this two-bit despot throw out your best chance of finding out what happened, to J. B. Carter?" This wasn't strictly true, since I had no more idea who helped the old man over the cliff than he did. But I had developed one or two little ideas that I couldn't do much about if Fischer gave me the boot. "You're the law here, aren't you?"

Grenby pivoted this way and that, ending up looking Fischer's way. "Hugo," he said, in a not very authoritative voice, "don't you think..."

"No, I don't," boomed Fischer. "I don't care what you do with this character, but I want him off my property—now! Take him, put him in jail. Put him under the jail, but get him away from me. If you have to bring him back, bring him in handcuffs. That's the only way I'll tolerate his presence in my house."

Jesus. Fischer really believed it. He wasn't just playing the guru; he'd taken out a patent on the role. And it looked as though nobody in this crowd was going to challenge him on my behalf. I was beginning to be sorry I'd said anything about my little visit with J.B. At least before I hadn't been a murder suspect.

"Goodey," Grenby started, "I'm going to have to..."

"Wait a minute," I said. I was going to go down with guns blazing. "I get an uneasy feeling, Mr. Fischer, that you couldn't care less who killed J. B. Carter. He was a nuisance to you, wasn't he? Aren't you the teensiest bit glad that you don't have him for a problem anymore?" Fischer wasn't going to answer me. He'd already turned his great head toward the mansion when somebody came out of the open front door.

"It's not true what this man says, is it, Hugo?" asked Emma Carter. She was still pale, and the skin around her eyes was drawn tight with grief, but she'd obviously bounced back fast. J.B. wasn't the only Carter who was made of durable stuff.

Fischer stopped short, and within a blink he'd changed gear and was a loving God, compassionate and all-caring. "Of course not, Emma," he said reaching out and taking both of her hands in his. The rest of us could have been in another state. Emma Carter had all of Fischer's attention. You could almost see it wash over her like soothing balm. "You know I care. We all share your loss."

Fischer reminded me of the slickest undertaker in the world about to sell her the solid walnut coffin with the bronze handles. But there was something in the set of Emma's jaw that told me that she couldn't quite book his act, either. Fischer was trying, in a genteelly compassionate way, to muscle her back through the doorway so that his thugs could wrap me up and leave me on the road for the garbage truck.

But Emma Carter wasn't being moved. She stood her ground against that juggernaut of compassion and certainty. It was easy enough for an outsider like me to sass the Great God Fischer. Win or lose, I wouldn't have to hang around to face his wrath. Now that she'd lost J.B., Mrs. Carter would probably need Fischer and The Institute more than ever.

But Fischer also wanted something from her, and Emma Carter's eyes said she hadn't forgotten who still owned the mansion. "Yes, I do know, Hugo, but I don't see what harm it can do for Mr. Goodey to remain here until..." she bit her lip and blinked hard, "...until the police find out who killed J.B. After all, Mr. Goodey may well have been the last person to talk to him. And if..."

Fischer knew an opportunity to back off a bit when he saw one. "Of course, Emma," he said. "If you think it would help for this man to stay for a while, he will. He's a nuisance, of course, but..." He made a generous gesture as if I were a present that was his to give.

"Thank you, Hugo," she said simply, and I felt that she meant it. Around there, even the right to say who stayed in your own house was a gift from Hugo Fischer. "And now I'd like to talk to Mr. Goodey alone."

"Right," I said eagerly, bounding up the steps. Fischer gave me an interesting look as I passed him, and Grenby said: "I'll want to talk to you when you're finished, Goodey."

Emma Carter led me through the entrance lobby of the big house, past the marble stairs and through an inconspicuous doorway I hadn't noticed in my tour of the mansion. "This used to be a sewing room," she explained as she turned on an overhead light, "but now I use it as a sanctuary when things get too hectic."

It was a small, comfortable-looking room, furnished with simple but expensive taste. Unlike what I'd seen of the rest of the mansion, it seemed a truly private room. There was no public-address box on the wall. Mrs. Carter gestured toward a small, overstuffed couch and we sat down knee to knee. I didn't say anything, figuring that she would come up with what was on her mind. She did.

"Mr. Goodey," she said, "I'm not so sure that I like you very much."

What could I say? Like J.B., she came to the point in a hurry, but at least she didn't try to hit me on the head.

"That's okay," I said. "Lately a lot of people seem to feel that way. Maybe I'm using the wrong toothpaste. But I don't think you brought me in here to say that."

"No, I didn't," she said. "But I believe in being honest. Do you?" She gave me a probing look, but nothing I couldn't handle.

"As often as possible," I said. "But if you're asking whether I'll tell you the truth, the answer is yes. I can't think of any reason to lie to you."

Her expression said she didn't think much of my limited candor, but she said: "Tell me about seeing J.B. last night."

So I did. Everything. When I told her how he slugged me with his sock of sand, she said: "Oh, that was terrible." But she couldn't totally repress a wry old smile. I assured her that the damage had been minimal and went on with my tale. She listened intently, not interrupting again until I'd told how J.B. had disappeared into the foliage and I'd come back down to the house.

Then she said softly: "It's such a shame." I thought she meant that it was a shame that he was dead, but then Emma went on: "If only J.B. could have trusted Hugo, there'd have been no need for him to hide out in that cave. He could still be here with..." She lowered her eyes.

"Do you really think so?" I asked. "I got a very strong impression that he'd rather have lived out there forever than come back down here and be Hugo Fischer's lap dog."

"Is that what you think I am, Mr. Goodey?" she asked with her chin up and her eyes firmly on mine.

"I haven't been around long enough to form an opinion on that," I said. "But your husband seemed pretty convinced that you'd gone soft in the head to even think of signing this place over to Fischer."

"To The Institute, Mr. Goodey," she corrected me. "To The Institute."

"From what I've seen so far," I said, "The Institute walks around inside Fischer's fancy moccasins. I haven't seen anybody else who seems to be more around here than a..." I remembered just in time that I was talking with a very nice old lady who'd just been violently widowed.

But Emma Carter wasn't going to let me get away with being chicken. "A flunky?" she asked with a probing look. "Is that what you meant to say, Mr. Goodey?"

"It'll do," I said. "This place doesn't seem to be over-crowded with people eager to spit in Fischer's eye. You're the first I've seen even bother to stand up to him."

She blushed a little as if she hadn't thought about it in exactly that way. "Hugo does tend to dominate at The Institute, Mr. Goodey," she said, "but I assure you that he is not nearly so autocratic as you seem to think. But that's not what I wanted to talk to you about. I get the feeling that you think that Hugo might be a suspect in my husband's murder. You don't really think that's possible, do you?"

"May I be completely honest?" I asked.

"That's all I ask of you."

"Then," I said, "even if I was impressed with Hugo Fischer, as the rest of you seem to be, there's no way that he wouldn't be a principal suspect. Ask yourself, who else stands to gain so materially from your husband's death?"

After a pause, she said: "I do, Mr. Goodey. I am J.B.'s sole beneficiary. I now own this estate entirely, as well as the rest of our property."

"I had thought of that," I admitted, "but who is really going to benefit? You're going to sign this place over to The Institute, aren't you?"

"Yes, I am," she said, positively enough. My silence must have been pretty eloquent, because Emma Carter felt the need to explain further. "Quite aside from my implicit faith in the honesty and sincerity of Hugo Fischer, Mr. Goodey, he has given me back my son. I suppose you know that Tommy spent the greater part of the last forty years in institutions?"

"Yes. J.B. told me. But he wasn't so sure that Fischer or The Institute deserved much of the credit."

"Well, I am sure," Emma said with determination. "I don't know exactly what it is, but there is something about the environment of The Institute which has greatly helped Tommy. I doubt very much that he will ever be any better, but he is at home and among people who love him. I can't ask for any more than that. To ensure that Tommy will always have a home, perhaps for many years after I am dead, I am going to give this estate to The Institute."

"Before the killer of your husband is found?" I asked, just to give the seed of doubt a little nourishment if it was there.

Emma was thinking over my question. That was something. "Even if I wanted to," she said, "I couldn't do it immediately. Not before the sheriff's investigation is finished and J.B.'s will goes through probate." I don't know what she read into my expression, but Emma then said: "Mr. Goodey, you seem to have involved yourself in my business quite a bit so far. Do you think you could go further and find out who killed J.B.?"

"That's not what I'm down here for," I said. "It may sound hard, Mrs. Carter, but it's none of my business. I came here to find out who killed Katie Pierce..."

"Do you think you could make it your business for five thousand dollars?"

"You don't have to pay me," my unbelieving ears heard me say, "I'll do whatever I can." That's the trouble with having been on the public payroll for so long, it dulled your commercial instincts. I was trying to think of some way to qualify that bit of altruism when Emma Carter said:

"No, Mr. Goodey, it would be worth more than that to me to find out who killed my husband. I'm a very rich woman, you know, even without my husband's estate."

"That's not what's bothering me," I said. "I'll be happy to accept your money, Mrs. Carter, if I'm successful. But are you sure that you'll be ready to accept what I find?"

She chewed that over for a minute and then looked me in the eye. "I'm sure, Mr. Goodey," she said. "Whatever you find out. Is it a deal?" She held out a graceful old hand toward me.

"It's a deal," I said as I took it.

15

When I came out of hiding with Emma Carter, Grenby and Harry Shearer grabbed me and hustled me into yet another small room, this one a former cloakroom. I was getting to know the mansion a lot better than I wanted to.

Shearer was in favor of breaking out the thumbscrews without a lot of time-wasting formalities. But Grenby was one of those new-breed cops who liked a little chat first. Besides, he was probably afraid of catching hell from Fischer if he splattered my blood on the floor.

With a bit of encouragement, I told them about my little visit with J.B. the night before. Neither of them wanted to feel the bump on the back of my head. Even words of sympathy were in short supply. So much for the mythical brotherhood of the law.

Despite the fact that I was probably the next to last person to see Carter alive, Grenby and Shearer didn't seem to be very impressed with the information I had to give them.

"You don't think it's even remotely possible?" I asked Grenby. "Remember that, from the cliff in front of his cave,

J.B. had an overview of the roof. He may have seen something."

"Yeah," said Shearer, "and I may be the mayor of San Francisco. If Carter had known anything that might have pinned the Pierce thing on somebody here, he'd have been down at headquarters singing like six canaries. He didn't know anything."

"Did you talk to him after Katie was killed?" I asked.

"Talk to him?" said Shearer. "As soon as he saw a uniform, he came storming down here prepared to swear to anything that would put Fischer and his flaky folk out on the curb looking for a home." If Harry was aware that Grenby was less than happy with his description of Fischer and The Institute, he didn't let on.

"But he didn't know anything?" I asked.

"Hell, he knew everything," Grenby said, "but what we wanted to know. If you listened to Carter, Fischer was Jack the Ripper, Al Capone and the guy who nobbled Judge Crater all in one. He knew so much, that if I'd had my way, he'd have been a star boarder in a laughing academy."

"Maybe you should have had your way," I said. "He'd be alive now, anyway."

Grenby cleared his throat to indicate that he hated to break up our intellectual conversation and then sent Harry out to make sure that his boys hadn't forgotten to pack anything for the trip back to Monterey. Harry said, "So long, Joe," but didn't break down at the prospect of leaving me. Then it was just Grenby and me in that cloakroom.

"Do I get the impression," I asked, "that Harry is going?"

"That's right," said Grenby. "Harry is going back to Monterey. When I need him, I'll send for him. Why?"

Grenby looked at me keenly, and I don't think he was trying to guess my weight.

"I just wondered," I said. "Harry may be a bit cynical, but he's a pretty good detective."

"So am I, Mr. Goodey," Grenby said. "I have a feeling that you think that I sent Harry away so that I could lose this case in some way, just sweep it under a convenient carpet until everybody forgot it. Is that right?"

I raised my eyebrows—I hoped not too expressively—and stayed mum.

"If you do, you're totally wrong. You couldn't be more wrong. I don't think there's anybody here who wants to find out who killed J.B. Carter more than I do. And I am going to find out."

"No matter who it is?"

"No matter," said Grenby positively. "I'd take Hugo himself out of here in cuffs if it turned out to be him."

I didn't believe him, and apparently neither did my face.

"You don't have to believe it," Grenby said without anger. "It's true. Goodey, neither you nor Shearer can understand what's happening here at The Institute. Hugo started it all, and he's the motivating force, but it's much bigger than even Hugo. There is something here, Goodey, that changes people's lives. I don't know what it is, but it certainly has changed mine. There's something almost magical here, Goodey, something precious."

"That could be, Lieutenant," I conceded, "but it seems to me that that's all the more reason for you to protect The Institute, even if it meant sliding over the little matter of who put an end to Katie Pierce and J.B. Carter."

He looked at me with more sorrow than anger. "It just doesn't work that way, Goodey," he said. "The Institute is built on truth, not lies and cover-ups. I did my best to find out what happened to Katie, and I'll do the same on this case. I have to. If I found out something and tried to hide it, it would be the same as trying to destroy The Institute."

He paused, pushed his glasses back in place with a forefinger and continued. "Besides," he said, "even if I wanted to bury this one, I couldn't. While you were talking with Emma, I got word that Sheriff Dominguez is taking a personal interest in this case. Apparently, Crenshaw got to him in some way. God knows how."

"Maybe he promised to get him elected governor of California. Or president. Or pope."

"Could be," said Grenby seriously. "But however he did it, my job—and my future—is on the line. Goodey, I'm an ambitious man. I always have been, but since I've been exposed to The Institute, my ambitions have changed. I believe that by using what we have here, the world can be changed for the better—on a large scale. And I can help do it. But it's not going to help me if Dominguez ties a can to me for allegedly protecting The Institute's good name. I've got to find out who killed J.B., Goodey, and I don't want you getting in my way. If you do, I'll take Hugo's advice and send you out of here in handcuffs."

"I'm sure you could," I said. "But I hope you won't have to. I seem to have picked up another job here. Emma Carter has hired me to find out who killed her husband." That really surprised him.

"Why, for Christ's sake?" he nearly shouted.

"Maybe she wanted a second opinion," I said. "She can afford the best, you know. But don't worry. I'll stay out from under your feet. I still haven't made a lot of headway in finding out who zapped Katie Pierce."

"You just stick to that one, Goodey," he said, "and we'll

all be a lot better off." He turned and walked out of the cloakroom.

I followed him out, but by the time I got to the foyer, Grenby was off in a corner kissing Harry Shearer goodbye, and nobody else seemed very interested in my existence. I considered looking Rachel up for a chat about old times, but after the confrontation of the night before, it seemed better to let the radioactivity count drop a bit first. I was wandering in the general direction of my room with the idea of staring at the ceiling for a while from a horizontal position when I heard my name called.

I turned around and Jack Gillette was coming my way with an amused expression on his face. "Well, Goodey," he said. "You seem to be making a lot of friends around here, but are you influencing people?"

"Not that I've noticed," I said. "But you seem to be bearing up pretty well under my lack of success."

"I do my best," he said.

"Tell me, Jack," I said, "do you still think I'm barking up the wrong guru? Do you subscribe to the theory that J. B. Carter bashed his own skull in and jumped off the cliff?"

"I don't believe in theories," he said. "Only answers. Are you coming up with any?"

"I'm working on some. What do you think of Rudolph Verrein?"

"As what? A suspect?"

"No, just in general."

"Rudy was all right," Jack said. "He just tried to go a bit fast and found that somebody had cut the ground out from under him. He got the idea that this is a social movement."

"Isn't it?"

"Nah," he said, "it's a nut house. Rudy forgot that."

"Is that why he got thrown out? I got the idea that it might have had something to do with Katie Pierce."

Gillette shrugged. "You get a lot of interesting ideas."

"You're not being a hell of a lot of help, Jack."

This accusation didn't seem to gnaw at his very being, but he said, "Tell you what, you seem to have a lot to think about, right?"

"You could say that."

"If it will help any, I'll tell you where I do all my best thinking."

"Where's that?"

"In the sauna. Downstairs in the basement. It's absolutely magic. As the sweat pours out of you, all your worldly problems dissolve. Everything becomes crystal clear. You'll probably come out of the sauna with the name of the murderer on the tip of your tongue."

"You guarantee it?" I asked.

"Double your money back," he said.

I remembered seeing a sauna bath during the tour the day before, and it didn't take me long to find the basement again. Actually, I just followed the steamy haze until I got to its source. It was the old-fashioned kind, constructed of stripped pine and made up of several airtight compartments, each with a separate door. Across the tile-floored hall was a shower room with a door to one side leading out to the deep end of the big swimming pool.

The little square windows to each of the compartments were opaque with steam, but the compartments all seemed to be empty. I stripped, hung my clothes on wall hooks, and took a thick towel from a pile on a slatted bench. The floor was cold and slightly gritty under my bare feet as I chose a compartment at random. The hot air hit me as I opened the door. I began to wonder if this were such a good idea, but pushed into the steamy fog and pulled the door closed behind me. Nearly blinded, I groped slowly across the wooden-slatted floor until my knees touched a bench.

As soon as I'd sat down in a blanket of tropical fog, I began to realize that Gillette had been wrong. A sauna bath was the last place I'd go for a nice, quiet think. Only someone with a frozen brain could think at all in such heat. Not to mention the boredom. It suddenly occurred to me that there's nothing to do in a sauna bath but sit and sweat. I could do that anywhere. I got to my feet and was reaching down for the towel when a voice from the burning mists in a far corner said: "Can't take it, eh, Goodey?"

I didn't have to strain to discover who my sauna mate was. It had to be Hugo Fischer or the devil, and I didn't think the devil could have taken the heat.

"Not at all, Mr. Fischer," I said, pretending to adjust the towel and sitting back down again. "I was just wondering whether the heat in this thing had gone off." I didn't want that pompous old fart to think that he could take something that I couldn't. Besides, I wasn't bored anymore.

I sat quietly just feeling the sweat trickling off me and wondering what would happen when all the liquid was gone. In the misty reaches of the sauna I could make out a dim shadow of Fischer. I think he looked his best in a thick fog.

"You think I'm just an old prick, don't you, Goodey?" he said. "Isn't that right?"

I couldn't resist saying: "You're not so old," but his snort told me he didn't think that was funny.

"Well, then," he asked, "what do you think?"

"I think you woke up one day and decided that you were God and have been trying to live up to the reputation ever since."

Deep inside his cloud, Fischer gave a divine sigh of mingled regret and disgust. "You know," he said, "you're all alike, you cops and reporters. You're so afraid that you'll believe in something, you close your tiny minds up like fists. Nothing can get in, and sure as hell nothing is going to get out."

"You're wrong," I said. "Grenby's a cop, and to hear him tell it you're the Messiah come to lead us all out of Egypt."

"Ah!" said Fischer, in modest triumph, "that's because Mike is no longer a policeman. He doesn't quite know it yet but he's on the verge of growing right out of that uniform. That gold badge is beginning to shrink, and it will go on shrinking until it completely disappears."

"I don't know," I said. "He just told me that he's prepared to lead you out of here in steel bracelets if that's the way the investigation goes. That sounds like a cop to me, not a disciple."

He thought that was funny, and he laughed through his nose at me.

"You were right to stop being a policeman, Goodey," he said. "You've got too much imagination, wrong-headed as it may be."

"I didn't jump," I said. "I was pushed. Like Katie Pierce."

He snorted again. He should have had that seen to. "For Christ's sake, Goodey," he said. "Are you still humming that old tune? You don't really think I had anything to do with Katie's death, do you? At the risk of sounding immodest, I don't kill people, I create them. Hell, I hardly knew Katie Pierce was around until she caused all this damned fuss by throwing herself off the roof."

"That was inconsiderate of her," I said.

"It sure as hell was," he said, stepping over my sarcasm.

"And now J.B. Carter hits himself over the head and throws his body off the cliff. I think he did it just to spite you. Is that what you're going to tell Grenby to find out?"

"J.B. Carter." He said the name ruefully. "You know something, Goodey? No matter how hard you try, there are some people you just can't help. J.B. was one, and I think you're another. It's a sad thing."

"I don't want your help any more than Carter did," I said. "Since I got here yesterday, I've seen what it did to Lennie and Barbara and Jack Willis. I can't afford that kind of help."

He seemed to think about that for a moment. All I could think about was how hot it was in that hellbox. It might have been my imagination, but I'd have sworn it was getting even hotter. Or maybe I just wasn't good sauna material. I could feel my mouth getting drier and drier, and my speech was slurring a bit. But I was determined not to say anything about the heat before he did, even if it did feel as though someone had set my face on fire.

"Jack Willis," Fischer said. Either my ears were melting or he was slurring his words a bit. "Shall I tell you a little bit about Jack Willis, Goodey?" I felt too weak to resist, so he rolled on. "Jack Willis first came down here as a hotshot newspaper reporter. To write about The Institute—about me. He thought he knew everything, but you know what, Goodey?"

I opened my mouth, but nothing came out but steam. My pulse was trying to escape through my head, and I was thinking more about several gallons of beer than about Jack Willis.

"Willis," Fischer went on, but slowly, "wasn't here for more than forty-eight hours before...before he knew that his life was a...fraud, Goodey. A f-fraud. And he literally

begged—begged me to let him...to let him...join...that is...
move into....whew..." Fischer made a painful swallowing
noise. I couldn't have agreed more.

"You know, Goodey," he said, "it's getting very...getting
very...in here..." The bench squeaked as he heaved his
considerable bulk from it. "I think I might just open the..."
He gave a deep sigh and then hit the floor like two hundred
pounds of wet baloney.

It dimly occurred to me that perhaps there was something going wrong. Either Fischer was a masochist, or this
sauna bath had taken a wrong turn. Putting both hands on
the bench at the sides of my legs, I gave a shove. Nothing
happened, except that my wet hands slipped off the boards
and I nearly joined Fischer on the floor. I didn't want to join
Fischer on the floor, so the next time I pushed a bit more
carefully, and after more effort than I thought possible,
found myself standing on my feet. At least I think they were
my feet. They were down there in the fog somewhere, and
when I leaned toward the sauna door they reluctantly came
with me. But very slowly.

I couldn't make a voice, but I mentally urged my legs,
one at a time, to carry me all the way over to the door with
the square little window. At that point, I was close enough
to fall to the door, but I knew that if I did, I'd never get up to
open it. So I waited for my legs, which waited for my feet,
and finally we all got to the door and deputized my right
arm to turn the knob. It did, and we all pushed on the door
together, but it didn't budge. At first, I thought I just didn't
have the strength left to push the door open. So I laid my
head against the window for a bit of a rest—the comparative
coolness of the glass was like a Caribbean cruise. Eventually, my eyes stopped rolling long enough to see that Tommy
Carter was on the other side of the glass leering at me with

idiotic good nature. His face was flattened on the window, further distorting his rubbery features, and his big shoulder was squarely against the outside of the door. I pushed with all my reduced might against the door but it was like leaning against a mountain. I tried shouting at Tommy, but all that came out was a gasping shriek that couldn't do justice to my well-chosen invective. I resorted to making menacing faces at him through the window, but that only inspired Tommy to screw up his face even more and press harder—if that were possible—against the door.

I gave up my efforts for a moment and just leaned against my side of the hot door, listening to my heart laboring like an oil pump sucking on a dry hole. With each stroke, a progressively constricting pain pythonned itself around my chest, making even shallow breathing not much fun. I felt as though someone was piling manhole covers on my chest one by loving one.

I looked through the little window again, hoping not to see Tommy anymore, but there he was. He hadn't changed a lot, and he was apparently still having a swell time. I thought about pushing on the door again, but was finding it hard enough just to keep my legs—which had somehow turned to rope—from collapsing. Soon, I found that the door was the only thing holding me up, and I clung to it like a vertical life raft, my cheek separated from Tommy's distorted face by only a sheet of glass. I began to fantasize that we were dancing cheek to cheek, and Tommy was leading.

Then my lolling, desperate eye caught on to something moving in from the side. The something turned into Jack Gillette floating toward Tommy as if in slow motion, then hitting Tommy's massive frame and bouncing awkwardly away like rubber on rubber. Nice going, Jack, I prayed. Try again. Jack got to his feet, but didn't make another rush. For a heartbeat I thought he'd given up a bad job. But then, after what seemed like an eternity, Gillette raised a clenched fist with deliberate slowness and launched it at Tommy's head. I watched the punch every inch of the way, and felt—rather than saw—it land squarely on Tommy's ear. The squashed face suddenly slid off the glass, and the door seemed to dematerialize as I fell through it onto the ice-cold white tiles outside.

I looked up several miles and saw a gigantic Jack Gillette standing over me sucking on the knuckles of his right hand. In a far corner, Tommy crouched with both big hands over his wounded ear. From his wide open mouth came the piercing, blubbery scream of a child in pain.

16

THERE WAS A HELL OF A LOT OF EXCITEMENT AFTER that. The basement suddenly got very full of people, with Don Moffitt in the middle of the mob shouting orders. Somebody kindly stacked me on a bench in the corner so I had a front-row view as about four of them lugged Fischer out of the sauna. They carried his naked bulk with great concern and caution, but Fischer was already beginning to struggle.

"For Christ's sake," he said. "I'm not dead yet. Let me down, you fools, let me down."

The boys looked a bit disappointed, but they put him down, and Fischer bobbed and weaved a bit to get his balance. He was flushed like an overcooked lobster, and in comparison his birthmark had paled. Somebody handed him a terrycloth robe, and Fischer was putting it on as he crossed the corridor and loomed over me. I didn't say anything, but just sat there shivering uncontrollably and feeling a bit silly because I was naked. I noticed that nobody handed me a robe.

"You know, Goodey," Fischer said, trying to control his

own shivering, "you may not be as crazy as I thought you were. What the hell happened here?" he snapped at Moffitt, who was hovering at his shoulder.

"My God, Hugo," Moffitt said distractedly, "I don't know. Gillette was on the way to his office and saw Tommy holding the door to the sauna shut and making a lot of noise. There was steam all over the fucking place. When he got closer, Jack saw that Goodey was trying to get out. He had to slug Tommy, and when he opened the door, Jack saw you collapsed on the floor. Apparently, Tommy turned the heat up as high as it could go. I—"

"What kind of a house are you running here, Moffitt?" Fischer cut in. "You claim you want real responsibility but when I give it to you, what happens? The village idiot just sort of drifts down here and tries to murder me. In my own house. Do you call that...?"

"I hate to tamper with your illusions, Mr. Fischer," I managed to say, "but how do you know it wasn't me that Tommy was trying to parboil?"

The thought had never occurred to him. I could see that. Fischer was turning it over in his mind like a curious gem, and he didn't like the idea of sharing the spotlight with anyone. Fischer would have tried to upstage the corpse at a funeral.

"You think so?" he said. Then without waiting for an answer, he snapped at Moffitt: "You find out what did happen. Get Grenby down here. And lock that moron up somewhere." Tommy had stopped howling and sat passively in the corner holding his ear and looking sorry for himself. Relieved to have something concrete to do, Moffitt bounded away, shouting orders at his minions.

By the time they rounded up Grenby, I was dressed again but still feeling pretty weary. I gave him what little information I could and left him in the basement doing some preliminary sleuthing. Grenby suggested that I get Carey to look me over. Apparently he was up in Hugo's quarters doing the same to the great man, but I gave it a pass. A little time flat on my back, I thought, would make a new man of me.

My room hadn't improved any, but the narrow bed had never looked better. Kicking off my shoes, I lay down and was preparing to hibernate when I became aware of a faint scratching at my door.

"Come in," I called. "If you have to." The door opened just a crack and in slid Genie Martin.

I was too tired to be very surprised.

"Well," she demanded, tiny hands on not-so-tiny hips, "aren't you happy to see me?"

"Genie," I said, "I'm absolutely delighted. Ecstatic. But I've just been steamed alive. You'll have to excuse me if I don't jump up and dance around the room."

"Yeah, I heard," she said, sitting down on the bed beside my legs. "You and the old man. That nut Tommy should have kept him in there until he melted away to a little spot of grease."

Here was candor I hadn't expected. I'd gotten so used to hearing Fischer's praises sung that my ears were ringing.

"Is that right?" I asked. "What would you and Old Man River do for a living then? Scratch for worms with the sparrows? Without Fischer, this place would fold up like a beach umbrella."

"I wish it would. Sometimes this place is worse than the slammer. Pops doesn't need it. There's a rich guy up in San Francisco who's been begging to set Pops up in his own drug-rehab joint. Pops is a charis-uh-charisma-type guy, you know. He's got personality."

"Sure," I said. "If I'm ever short of a book end, I'll keep him in mind. But tell me, what do you make of Tommy Carter? Has he ever tried to hurt anybody before?'"

"That dummy?" Genie said. "Nah. Oh, he's strong enough. He could hurt you without trying. But he's usually so dopey that he just wanders around mumbling to himself. Occasionally, you know, he gets a bit wild, but it never lasts long. Somebody in the house just puts the arm on him and calls Jim Carey. Before too long, Tommy is just as happy and jerky as before. Sometimes I wish I was that happy."

"You're not going to make anyone happy hanging around up here with me. You're taking big chances, even if you did get away with it last night. Didn't Pops wonder where you'd been?"

"Yeah," she said, running an idle hand up my leg, "but it was no big problem. I shot him that line you told me about waking up before he did, and he bought it. He wasn't all that happy, but he didn't have much choice." She looked very young and very smug.

"Maybe not, but you're pushing dumb luck a bit far. What do you want to do, help me commit suicide? If Pops is so charismatic—"

"That's the word!"

"—why aren't you somewhere bathing in his ruby-red glow instead of up here risking my health?"

"That's not exactly what I'm looking for," she admitted girlishly, at the same time walking her fingers up my leg to my groin and getting a good grip.

I raised my head slightly to watch the action. "I'm pretty sure you're wasting your time there," I said. "I don't think anybody's home." A little bird told me that that wasn't strictly true, and something seemed to hint the same thing to Genie.

"Let's just see," she giggled, clutching at the pull on my zipper.

The zipper came down just as Rachel Schute came through the door of my room. Without knocking.

"Joe," Rachel began, "I just wanted to..."

She stopped to take in the pretty scene on my bed. I was looking as nonchalant as a man with a gaping fly can, and Genie had set a new record for the sitting broad jump and was poised like a cat at the foot of the bed. When she saw that it was Rachel, and not Pops, her expression veered from terror to malice. To her warped little mind this constituted a woman-to-woman confrontation with Rachel.

Rachel pretended that Genie wasn't there. "I was going to ask if you were okay, Joe," she said. "But I guess I don't have to now." She slipped me a meaningful look.

"Sure, I'm fine, Rachel," I said. "I just got a bit overheated." I then blushed, and Rachel couldn't keep from smiling. "Thanks for being concerned. You shouldn't have bothered."

"I know," she said crisply. She started to go but then turned back. "By the way, Hugo's holding a memorial service for J.B. on the lawn in ten minutes." Then, as an afterthought, Rachel gave Genie a direct look and said: "In case you're interested, Genie, your husband is looking for you."

Then she was gone. Genie followed her without even offering to zip up my trousers. I lay back down on the bed. But somehow the urge to sleep had fled. I was feeling restless. I could always go to the memorial service, but it occurred to me that this might be a good chance to get a more thorough look at that area around J.B.'s cave.

I took some caution to slide around the crowd forming for the memorial service and the security guards, who seemed to have suddenly increased in number, but once I had gained the woods I made very good time. My super sauna with Fischer didn't seem to have had any lasting effect, but nonetheless I was puffing heavily by the time I got to the cliff near the cave and had to stop and wait for the knot in my side to relax its death grip. While I waited, I cautiously peeked at the memorial service, which had begun by this time. Even from that height, I could make out the figure of Hugo Fischer, in the middle as usual, and hear snatches of a slow, mournful song.

The mouth of the cave had been completely uncovered by Grenby's men, and they'd removed J.B.'s meager hermit's gear. There was nothing but a bunch of trampled shrubbery and a hint of lingering B.O. to suggest that he'd ever been there. What a way for a millionaire to end. But maybe J.B. would have preferred to go that way to spending his dotage on Fischer's lap. He'd been a gutsy old man even if he did hit from behind.

After poking among the rubble on the floor of the cave and coming up with nothing more interesting than mummified orange peel, I stepped back out into the dying sunlight and tried to get the big picture. It didn't prove very enlightening at first. There's something so blank about an empty cave. It doesn't tell you a lot. I knew I should have stayed awake in geology class.

But then I saw something on the left-hand side of the cave mouth that brought me closer—a shallow egg-shaped notch about as high as my chest. It could have been a natural formation, but something made me doubt it. That same something left me climbing among the branches of a squat pine growing hard by the right side of the mouth of the cave. There, behind the thick-needled branches, I found what I hadn't had enough sense to be looking for. That old son of a bitch, I thought, and climbed out of the branches. There didn't seem to be anything more to do there, so I began walking along the cliff toward the mansion.

By the time I got back down to the lawn, the memorial service was breaking up, and I joined the crowd drifting toward the mansion. I was about to go into the mansion when a big car pulled into the parking lot. It was a brand new Lincoln Continental, as white as an albino snowman, with a blue light on the roof. More law.

But not just any law. Painted on the car door in flowing script beneath a big gold star was: Luis de Redondo y Dominguez, Sheriff of Monterey County. The mountain had come to Mohammed. This was something I wanted to see.

But so far the back doors of the Continental were still shut, and no Sheriff Dominguez had emerged. I strained my eyes but couldn't penetrate the black one-way glass of the car's window. I knew he could see me all right, but I didn't think he was bothering. And there was no Hugo Fischer in sight, either. What there was, was Don Moffitt, looking very rock-jawed, marking parley with a sheriff's sergeant in a skin-tight gabardine uniform, a muscular giant who could have worn Moffitt for a watch fob. But just then the sergeant was leaning on the half-opened driver's door, eyeless behind mirrored sun glasses, and explaining that his boss man wanted to have a little chat with the head man of this-uh-organization.

Moffitt started bristling like a kicked Doberman, but just then the great man himself swept up, flanked by Dr. James Carey and Pops Martin. Mike Grenby was of Fischer's party, but once he saw Dominguez's car, he started detaching himself and looking professional. Sensing that he was the perfect emissary between these potentates, Grenby moved forward to powwow with the sheriff's pet tiger.

I didn't hear what Grenby said, but it won him the right to stoop down and talk with somebody in the hidden back seat. He couldn't have said a lot, because in about twenty seconds, Grenby backed away, and the sheriff's driver was diving into the breach and pulling the back door open with a flourish.

And out came Luis de Redondo y Dominguez, Sheriff of Monterey County. There should have been a roll of drums, blare of trumpets, but there wasn't. It's hard to slide out of a car with a great deal of dignity, but Dominguez came close. The sergeant mentally lifted him to the ground without daring even to touch his sleeve. It wasn't until the sheriff was standing beside the car that I realized how tall he was. Or how small. He looked like a mummified Boy Scout, a little brown man with mestizo features ravined with about seventy years' worth of deep furrows running down to a faultless khaki shirt collar. In place of a tie he had about half a pound of silver-mounted turquoise on a leather thong. An ivory-gripped .44 Magnum in a tooled holster gave him a permanent slope to port.

Dominguez was interesting enough, but then Frederick M. Crenshaw followed him out of the car with an expression of worried triumph on his face. He glanced at me defiantly, as if I told him he shouldn't be there—which he shouldn't—and stood looking around at the mansion grounds as if he'd just bought them.

I'd half expected Fischer to order Dominguez and Crenshaw thrown into the moat, but instead he shucked off Carey and Pops and beamed in on the sheriff with hand outstretched and a smile he'd never shown me. I hadn't missed much. I drifted along to one side, eager to witness this historic confrontation.

I was just out of earshot, but I didn't have to read lips to make out Fischer's message: Dominguez was more than slightly welcome at The Institute. The sheriff accepted that intelligence without blinking, let his old monkey's paw be swallowed up by Fischer's hands, and indicated with a twist of his head the presence of his good friend, Fred Crenshaw. Fischer wasn't quite so effusive with Crenshaw, but he took it like a man, and with a sweeping gesture indicated that Dominguez and his party should accompany him up to the ranch house for the non-alcoholic equivalent of a shot of red eye.

Dominguez scotched that suggestion with very few one syllable words, gave Crenshaw a dry handshake and was burrowing back into the Continental before Fischer even knew he'd been given the bird. The big sergeant closed the door after him as if shutting a jewel casket and leapt for the driver's seat. The Continental turned in a little over its own length and was gaining speed when it suddenly stopped. One smoky rear window slid down about three inches, and Dominguez's wrinkled mug appeared through the crack. Grenby sprang to the car and lent an attentive ear. The window zipped up, and the car spurted ahead leaving Grenby with his head still cocked.

Fischer picked up his jaw, gathered the folds of his tattered dignity around him, and hot-footed it for the mansion with Moffitt, Carey and Pops in close pursuit.

I asked a distracted Grenby: "What did the generalissimo want?"

Grenby regarded me bleakly: "Results. Right now." With that he took off for the mansion at a near run, probably to try to do something about Fischer's dented self-esteem. I couldn't imagine there had been any permanent damage. It would take more than a snub from an ancient Spaniard to pierce that horny hide.

That pretty much left me and Crenshaw alone in the parking area. Crenshaw looked a little less sure of himself now that the Godfather had left him on his own.

I wandered over to where he stood. "You know how to pick your transportation," I said. "How much did that little ride cost you?"

"That's none of your business," Crenshaw snapped, showing that there was still a bit of pop on his fast one. "What progress have you got to report?"

"Not much," I said. "As Dominguez probably told you, there was somebody else killed here last night. J.B. Carter, the owner of this place. That sort of interests the sheriff's department in The Institute again. But I'm not much closer to finding Katie's killer. Maybe the sheriff's man will tumble over him in the dark."

"That's what I'm paying you for, Goodey," he said. "Do you know whether Fischer knows about Katie's new will yet?"

"If he does," I said, "he hasn't mentioned it to me. But he might to you, now that you've decided to drop in like his."

Crenshaw shifted his weight from one leg to the other. I knew damned well that he didn't know what to do next, and I wasn't in a hurry to come to his rescue. I didn't much like the idea of Crenshaw coming down to lean on my shovel. I didn't think his presence was going to help my relations with Fischer. If anything could.

"Listen, Goodey," he said, looking about as wretched as he knew how, "I know I shouldn't have come down here. I couldn't help it. Last night I got word that Dominguez would talk to me if nothing more. I met him this afternoon, and when he offered to bring me here personally, I just couldn't refuse."

"Well," I said, unrelenting, "you're here now. What are you going to do that I can't? Maybe you'd like me to check out so that you can go it alone. What kind of detective do you think you'd make, Mr. Crenshaw? I don't know why you bothered to hire me in the first place." I didn't go so far as to offer him his money back.

"Christ," I went on, "you could have come back here anytime, don't you know that? They've been dying to get their hands on you to try to convert you to The Institute's way of thinking. Don't think that riding down here on Dominguez's shirttails has done you any lasting good. Especially after your *padrone* just stomped all over Fischer's blue suede shoes."

"I really didn't think..." Crenshaw started, but I decided to exercise some of my famous compassion.

"Come on," I said. "Let's go into the house and see if we're still welcome." It was near dark by then, and the old mansion was lit up and seemed inviting compared to the cool sea mist that had started rolling in.

Nobody tried to bar our way at the front door, and when we got into the big room hung with all the slogans, a crowd of residents swarmed around the large bulletin board. Jack Gillette stood to one side with a knowing look on his face. He took in Crenshaw's presence without comment.

"What's up?" I asked.

"See for yourself," Jack said. "I hope you're feeling strong."

Intrigued, I muscled my way through the gawkers and

found what had gotten them so excited. It was a notice, freshly typed:

Hugo has called a megathon for 2400 hours tonight. The below listed will appear in the Horizon Room at that hour:

Lenore Fischer
Pops Martin
James Carey
Harold Fischer
Don Moffitt
Jonah Goodey
Rachel Schute
Genie Martin
Emma Carter
Susan Wallstrom
Mark Kinsey
Aileen Moffitt
Michael Grenby
Frederick Crenshaw

The notice went on to list a large number of lesser beings who weren't included in the megathon but who apparently had some function to perform. One of the few names I recognized was that of Jack Gillette.

When I walked back over to him, Gillette was smiling broadly.

"Do you know what a megathon is, Joe?" he asked.

"I've got a general idea," I said. "And I'm going to catch some sleep." I turned to Crenshaw, who was looking bemused. "Jack will find you a room," I told him. "See you at midnight."

17

I WAS SUDDENLY WIDE AWAKE. MY WATCH ON THE bedside table told me that it was five minutes to midnight. No sooner had I swung my feet to the floor than a peremptory knock hit the door, and two characters in shapeless blue gowns came in and turned on the overhead light. They were a couple of mugs I'd seen hanging around downstairs, and in the gowns they looked like they were going to a Mafia Halloween party. But they seemed to be taking the whole thing very seriously.

I reached for my trousers, but one of them said: "You won't need those." The other one held out his arms, on which was folded something of purest white.

"What's that?" I asked.

"Your robe."

"Are you kidding?"

"No," he said. "All participants in a megathon wear these robes. It's part of the ritual." He shoved the robe toward me.

I shrugged, took the robe from him and slipped it over my head. There was no mirror in the room, but I imagined that I looked lovely. The other one held out a pair of Japanese-style sandals and I put them on.

"What," I said, "no turban?" But neither of them even cracked a smile.

I started to put on my watch, but one of them said: "Leave it. You won't need it." For some reason, I obeyed.

"Follow us, please."

I did. And as we came out into the half-darkened hall, I saw another white-robed figure turning ghostlike down the stairs. I couldn't tell who it was. I followed my guides down the stairs to the same room to which I'd been summoned the night before. But the Horizon Room had changed. For a start, the lights were out, and the room was dimly lighted entirely with tall, white candles. All the furniture had been removed, and a circle of large cushions left in place of it. Most of the cushions had white-robed figures on them, but in the dimness it wasn't easy to make out who they were.

My attendants led me to a cushion on the side of the circle near the door and indicated that I should sit down. Then they stepped back against the wall. The cushion on one side of mine was empty, but the other was occupied by Aileen Moffitt. She was sitting in a modified lotus position and seemed to be communing with the verities with little spare time for neighborly chitchat.

I turned my head to see Rachel sitting down on the empty cushion to my left. I whispered, "What's the schedule?"

"You'll find out, Joe," she said, in less than a whisper. "Just relax and let it happen."

Since I didn't have much choice, I took her advice. The gaps in the circle were filling in. As my eyes adjusted to the light, I could see that Pops Martin and Genie had come in and taken places across the room, leaving only two empty cushions directly across from my position. I had an idea who these were for.

Then all the white-clad figures were standing up, some more gracefully than others, and, not to be a spoilsport, I joined them. All eyes in the room seemed to turn in my direction, but I knew they weren't looking at me. By turning my head slightly, I could see that Lenore Fischer had entered the room and was heading for one of the two empty places. She stopped behind a cushion with her eyes riveted on the door behind me.

I could have turned and watched the door, but instead I watched Lenore Fischer's face. It seemed totally blank, but then, at once, her face took on life, and, almost as if it were a mirror, I could see reflected in it Fischer's presence in the doorway. Her eyes followed Fischer as he slowly walked around the circle to my left and stood behind the only remaining empty cushion. He took Lenore's hand, and as if on command, all of the rest of us in the circle joined hands with those on either side. I didn't will my hands to move; they just did. Rachel's hand was warm—and slightly damp. Aileen's was as dry and cool as marble. In his white robes, Fischer took on Olympian stature. There was dignity in his flawed face that was not assumed. There was no question who was in command in that room. His robe was no different from any of the others, but he wore it with absolute authority. I couldn't say that I liked the feeling. Sitting there in my underwear in that unaccustomed garment, I felt very vulnerable.

"Let us sit, friends," said Fischer, and we did. My knees cracked loudly, and Rachel gave me a cautionary look as if I'd fired them off on purpose.

As we sat, the blue-robed functionaries blew out most of the candles and disappeared. The door closed behind the last of them, and it was as if the room, and all of us in it, were cut off completely from the rest of the world. As if there were nothing but a void on the other side of that door. I didn't much like the feeling.

Out of the near darkness, Fischer's voice, deep, mellow and somber, said: "As those of you who have attended a megathon will know, we always begin with a period of total silence to empty our minds, to cleanse our faculties of outside influences. Let the silence begin."

And it did. Not that it had been all that noisy before, except for a certain amount of restrained coughing and clearing of throats. Now complete silence fell over the room, and I was afraid of even swallowing too vigorously for fear of making someone fall out of a trance. The others may have been emptying their minds, but I was busy trying to figure how I could turn Fischer's megathon to my own advantage. I wasn't quite sure exactly what he was out to accomplish. It was probably to get me and Crenshaw off his back and somehow help Grenby satisfy Dominguez. That was a tall order even for a megathon, and I was going to be watching with interest.

But I suspected that I was going to be more than an observer at this clambake. With the knowledge I had picked up at J. B. Carter's cave, I figured I could at least enliven matters a bit if they threatened to get dull. I had a feeling that this was going to be an unusual megathon.

I got a bizarre image of J.B. at the megathon in which he'd starred, sitting perched on one of those cushions with his white beard jutting out over those flowing robes like a renegade monk. He must have been as full of anticipation as I was at that very moment. The mandatory silence wasn't very exciting, but I wasn't exactly eager to have it end.

"Somebody is not concentrating," Fischer rapped out,

and I wondered if I'd involuntarily let out a snort at the mental image of J.B. under the gun. A barely audible but impatient sound coming from Rachel's direction gave me the idea that maybe I had. I silently vowed to be a better boy in the future, but I couldn't help looking around the circle.

It wasn't easy to make out much in that light, but most of them seemed to be sitting and staring blankly into the near darkness. I was finding it a bit hard to keep my own eyes open and to stifle the yawns that came rolling up from my throat.

I tried to fight them off by mechanically moving my eyes from one person in the circle to the other. Genie was at Pop's left, and the white robe made her look more like a depraved pixie than ever, although it wasn't nearly as becoming as the sweet nothing she'd worn to my room.

I wondered whether Fischer could detect impure thoughts during a megathon.

Across the circle from Genie, Emma Carter sat with all the serenity of the lead soprano in a hard-shell Baptist choir. It seemed pretty obvious that she was drawing considerable support from Fischer and the others, but I found it hard to believe that J.B. wasn't dominating her thoughts no matter what Fischer said. It would be interesting to see whether Fischer had the chutzpah to bring up the matter of signing over the estate during the megathon.

Before I could move my survey to the next cushion, the lights of the room began to grow brighter like a false dawn. Pops Martin jumped as if someone had stuck him with a pin. I looked around at a few faces, and I imagined that I wasn't the only one who felt a bit disoriented. I noticed that the anti-Hugo graffiti had been covered with a sheet.

"Friends," said Fischer, winning all our attention, "for the purposes of this megathon, I want you to forget all about time. The megathon is timeless and so, for as long as you are in it, are you. I shall establish the time reference that we will use. And it is now time for breakfast."

The door opened and a squad of blue-robed minions under the direction of Jack Gillette came into the room bearing large covered trays. One rolled a cart loaded with plates and metal serving dishes. In a very short time, we were all eating bacon and eggs and chatting with our neighbors as if it were 9 A.M. and not the middle of the night.

Rachel seemed to have declared a truce with me.

"This is my first megathon, Joe," she said, with the shining eyes of a girl at the junior prom.

"Me, too," I said, a bit fatuously. "Rachel," I said, "will you tell me something?"

"Of course, Joe," she said sincerely.

"What are you wearing under your robe?"

I shouldn't have done that. Rachel's mouth went as tight as a triple bigamist's schedule. "Joe," she said piercing me with scornful eyes, "you're impossible," and dove back into her coffee cup.

I finished my breakfast trying to look penitent. Before I could ask for a second cup of coffee, the dishes had been whisked away, and Hugo Fischer had a vise-grip on our attention. There was no question who was running this séance.

"Although not always successful," Fischer said, "the period of silence with which we traditionally begin a megathon is intended to purge the mind of inconsequentials, to scour it of the petty concerns of everyday life. In cases where there *is* a rational faculty," he said with a slightly sardonic smile as he raked the circle with his powerful eyes, "it is often beneficial." Some sycophant chuckled, and I allowed myself a grim smile.

"But what of the soul?" Fischer said, in the rising tones of an orator. "How shall we cleanse it? How, indeed?"

This wasn't a question that had kept me up nights, but my fellow megathoners were taking it to heart. Nobody said anything. I don't think they were meant to. I certainly didn't raise my hand.

"*Howwwww?*" Fischer ululated the word at the ornate ceiling like a fleshy wolf. If I'd known, I'd have been glad to tell him, if only to get him to stop doing that.

When he was finally pretty sure that he had all our attention, Fischer said: "Nobody knows? I'll give you a hint. Did not the Apostle James say 'Confess ye, one to another'?"

If he did, he didn't say it to me, but the rest of our company bobbed their collective chins up and down like a bunch of drinking birds. I tried to look noncommittal. I glanced at Crenshaw, and he looked bewildered by the entire proceeding. Perhaps symbolically, he still had a bit of egg yolk on the sides of his mouth.

"Well, then," Fischer said, "suppose we have a little session of true confessions just to steam-clean those psyches, shall we?" He looked around the circle with a faintly predatory eye. "Who will start?"

This was more like it. I looked around the room as eagerly as Fischer did. Right. Let's have it. One or two confessions of murder, by the numbers. At last, Fischer and I were in accord. All we wanted was a teensy-weensy confession, and we could all go back to bed. I imagined that was what Grenby wanted, too.

But we were all disappointed. Nobody said anything. Not a word. Somebody was not cooperating.

"Well?" demanded Fischer, and he spoke for both of us, "doesn't anybody have anything to confess? Nothing? Am I living, among saints? Have I died and gone to heaven. Do I—"

Fischer stopped short because Aileen Moffitt had silently gotten to her feet and was standing in front of her cushion. Her eyes were on the floor.

"Yes, Aileen?" Fischer said, and his voice was suddenly the essence of gentleness. Don Moffitt looked stricken; his eyes were locked on the slim form of his wife.

"I have a confession to make, Hugo," she said in a mechanical monotone. She was still looking at the carpet. "I want to confess. I want to confess to—to..."

She paused as if weighed down by our eyes, but I don't think she was aware of anyone but Fischer. He said nothing more, but waited patiently for her to continue. Slowly, Aileen raised her eyes until they were on Fischer's face. Her expression was tense, controlled.

"I've been ungrateful, Hugo," she continued. "To you, to The Institute, to all my brothers and sisters. I have been trying to make Don leave The Institute. I wanted a home of my own, all the stupid little things people in the outside world have. I wanted them."

Aileen looked down as if she were finished, but soon raised her eyes again. "But I wanted more than that," she went on. "Much more. I wanted Don to leave here...to leave you...to get out because...because you are killing him. Killing him as a man!"

Moffitt flinched but said nothing.

"It's true, Hugo," she continued, apparently not so much confessing as justifying her heresy. "When he's in your shadow, Don's not a man. He's a boy—a child in your house. You call him the vice-president, but there is no vice-president of The Institute. Because there is only one man here, and that's you, Hugo, just you. The rest of us are only children."

An amazed silence settled on the circle. Even Fischer didn't seem to know what to do with this accusation which had crept up on him disguised as recantation. He looked at Don Moffitt, but Moffitt seemed to be waiting for the meaning of Aileen's words to soak through his skull to his brain.

Aileen saved him the trouble.

"But I forgot," she said, continuing as if there had been no pause. "I forgot these." She raised her hands palms up, and the flowing sleeves of her robe fell back, revealing the insides of her elbows. She was talking about the ghosts of ancient needle tracks on the veins of her dead-white inner arms.

"I forgot that when I came here," she said, "my whole life—my whole death—was shooting poison into these as fast as I could find a vein. I forgot that I was turning tricks with anybody Don could find so that we could get more dope. I forgot that when I came to your door even the baby I was carrying in my body—little Donny—had been poisoned by the shit I was sticking in my arm. He was *born* a hype."

She said this impassively as if she were talking about somebody else's life. As if she were telling a story. "I forgot," she continued, "that if it weren't for you, I'd probably be dead now. And Don, too, or at least in prison. And there would be no Donny. We owe you our lives, Hugo. Our lives. I forgot that. And I'm sorry." Aileen lowered her arms to her sides. She took an uncertain step toward Fischer and began to cry. Her thin face was like a crumpled mask, and tears left little streaks of mascara on her flat cheeks. She took another step.

With a strangled sound in his throat, Moffitt jumped to

his feet. I wondered if anyone else noticed Fischer catch his wrist in a powerful grip and hold him back. Most must have been watching Aileen as she took a third step, stopped and started to sway. Even I started to unwind from my cushion, but before I could, Fischer was up—with Moffitt at his shoulder—and had caught Aileen before she could fall. Gently, he took her weight on his arms and let his thick legs bend until they were both kneeling with Mofitt poised over them just half a step too slow.

"It's okay, Aileen," Fischer said, stroking her hair. "I understand. Hugo understands." Shifting her weight to his left arm, Fischer reached back and pulled Moffitt to a kneeling position, too. Moffitt put his arm around Aileen's shoulders. The three were frozen in the middle of the circle like figures out of an illustrated Bible: God forgiving the sinners.

I won't say that mine were the only dry eyes in the room, but all of the women were having hanky trouble, and some of the men looked suspiciously moist. Even old Crenshaw looked as though somebody had hit him with a sneak punch.

Eventually, Fischer stood up over the kneeling figures of Don and Aileen as if about to announce his next miracle. Then Moffitt helped his sobbing wife over to his cushion, and Fischer completed the circle again. His face said that he had things back under control.

A heavy silence fell over the room, broken only by Aileen's muffled whimpers. Soon, even those subsided, and tension began to build up again. I wondered who would be the next turn.

Close to the last thing I expected to hear was Rachel's husky voice say: "Hugo, I have a confession to make, too." I turned, noting her calm expression and determined eye. She went on, ignoring me: "I have failed in my responsibility to the house and to my brothers and sisters."

I thought I detected a minute glance in my direction before she said: "Hugo, I failed to tell you that this afternoon, when I went up to Joe Goodey's room, Genie Martin was there. And I'm pretty sure she was there last night, too."

18

HAVE YOU EVER HAD THE FEELING THAT SOMEBODY HAD snuck up behind you and quick-frozen your brain? Mine was thirty degrees below zero and getting more numb by the second. Hundreds of little men were busily packing it with dry ice and whistling while they worked.

Everyone else in the happy circle seemed to be feeling the same. Rachel's bombshell had frozen us where we sat. Years from then they would find us, fifteen skeletons in a circle of rotted cushions, and would wonder what evil demon had bewitched us. But then, Fischer, like the wizard he passed for, broke the spell by swiveling his great head, first toward Genie, then toward me. Then back to Genie.

I wasn't sorry. With perhaps typical chauvinism, I was perfectly happy to sacrifice Genie to win a little time. Besides, I wasn't paying too much attention to either Fischer or Genie. My eyes were on Pops. I'd suspected him of dozing slightly through Aileen Moffitt's histrionics, and even now he was a bit slow coming to life considering the magnitude of the cat that Rachel had just let out of the bag.

But I suspected that he'd come roaring back, and I wanted to be ready to jump the right way.

Fischer saved us both the trouble.

"Genie," he boomed, "is what Rachel says true?"

Genie's sharp little face was a maelstrom of emotion as she obviously weighed the options available to her: deny, cry, confess, run for it or come out counterpunching. Something whirred behind her bright eyes as she chose one.

Genie all but flew up from her cushion as she zeroed in on Rachel. "You're just jealous," she spat. "You pitiful, dried-up old moneybags. You couldn't get him (meaning me) even with all your fucking cash, but you keep hanging around like a bitch in heat. You'd better get Rachel a real man," she advised Fischer, "before she rapes a snake."

That wasn't exactly the reaction anybody had been expecting, but it was effective. That overdose of truth venom sent Rachel scrambling up the nearest tree. She just wasn't in the same league with Genie when it came to gutter fighting. It even set the others back for a moment, but not for long. Before Genie had time to savor her victory a storm of abuse broke over her head.

I won't bother to catalogue the different kinds of whore Genie was called. It tended to get a bit repetitious after the first few minutes, anyway. But surprisingly, this cascade of denunciation seemed to affect Genie about as much as the confetti had at her wedding. When the mob paused to refill their quivers of invective, she jumped back into the fray with both stack-heeled little feet.

"What the hell did you expect?" she demanded, turning on Pops, who'd said hardly a word. I think he was genuinely surprised and even hurt. "You're nothing but a broken-down old phony who couldn't even get it up on the Fourth of July. You lay around here trying to letch off all the chicks, but those days are gone, grandpa. You'd better stop thinking you can suck up youth from me or any other young chick, because you can't."

Then Genie compounded the heresy by switching her attack to Fischer. "But it's not really Pops' fault," she cried, "it's yours, Hugo. You're so grateful for his loyalty you'd do anything to keep Pops happy. Even pimp for him. Pops likes young girls? Okay, here's the message: Hey, girlie, you want to serve The Institute and Hugo? Go throw a fuck on Pops Martin. It's no big thing. Nothing is too good for Pops, right?"

Genie pivoted around the circle as if we were all going to jump her. That wasn't the most remote possibility I could think of. She was slinging unvarnished truths around like hand grenades, and the impact wasn't much less shattering. Pops sat there looking destroyed. He couldn't bring himself even to look at his young bride. Fischer, who wasn't even supposed to be at a loss for words, couldn't seem to find the right ones just then.

"Bullshit!" Genie cried. "I crawled in here out of the gutter, but I'm not a slave. I'm not a thing, a gift, you can give your old pal, Pops. I may have been a whore, but I'm not anymore, and even if I was I'd decide who I'd sell myself to." She turned to face Fischer defiantly. "And if you don't like it, Hugo, you can go fuck yourself!"

She balanced there staring into Fischer's face as if she expected to be struck by lightning. Fischer didn't say anything, just raised his flushed face and stared at her impassively. She held his gaze for perhaps thirty seconds, but then broke and bolted through the circle to the door.

We all stared at the door as it slammed behind her. But only Lenore Fischer got up from her pillow and started to follow.

"Let her go," said Fischer peremptorily, but Lenore kept moving. Soon she had her hand on the doorknob. "Lenore," said Fischer. Then more sharply: "Lenore!" But she opened the door and was gone. The door closed gently behind her, but the click rang like a gunshot in the stillness she left behind.

Then Fischer swiveled his big head toward me and said, as if none of the last ten minutes or so had happened: "Mr. Goodey, how is it that you choose to return our hospitality by trying to rape one of our young women—and her on her honeymoon, too?"

This was about the last thing anybody expected him to say, and after a massive intake of breath, there was a thunderclap of shocked laughter. It wasn't really that funny, but the relief from tension was so great that they sat there and roared. It was more hysteria than laughter. I wasn't even involved with The Institute, but I'd found Genie's little revolt a disturbing experience. Fred Crenshaw seemed to be having the same reaction, only more so. His face was ashen.

Finally, after several spasmodic resurgences, the laughter died down, leaving in its wake a little pool of exhausted calm, broken only by the occasional stifled titter or gasp. Fischer seemed content to let the vacuum exist for a while, but it seemed to me that this might be my moment.

"I wonder," I said as offhandedly as I could manage, "whether any of you would be interested in knowing how J.B. Carter died?"

Cousin Harold let out an unintentional shout of laughter, but then all was silence. Twenty-four eyes were trained on me. And serious.

"That's not very funny, Goodey," Fischer growled. "You ought—"

"It wasn't meant to be," I said. "I meant just what I said.

I know how J.B. died."

"What the hell do you think you're trying to pull off?" demanded Mike Grenby, suddenly realizing that he was the law around there and that I was treading deep into his territory. "If you've got information—"

"Let him speak, Mike," said Emma Carter quietly.

"I probably should have told you this in private, Mrs. Carter," I said, "but I won't try to keep you in suspense. As Lieutenant Grenby would probably have discovered tomorrow anyway, your husband wasn't murdered. He was caught in a booby trap that he had set at the mouth of that cave of his."

I'd expected them to be surprised, and they didn't let me down. Even after the recent emotional bombardments, my revelation could be considered more than mildly interesting. I watched especially Emma's face. There were tears in her eyes, but her predominant expression was one of relief. That may sound strange, but I think she'd been genuinely worried that one of The Institute's muscle heads had killed J.B. in a burst of misguided loyalty to Fischer.

"Are you sure, Mr. Goodey?" she asked me.

"As certain as I can be," I said. "Was J.B. a very strong man?"

"For his age," she said, "yes he was. He'd worked hard all his life."

"I thought so," I said. Grenby was getting more and more curious and impatient. Fischer didn't look like he'd wait much longer, either, so I decided to just spit it out. "What happened," I said, speaking to the group, "was that J.B. was afraid that someone from down here would sneak up on him while he was sleeping. As a deterrent, he pulled a resilient tree limb across the mouth of the cave and fixed it into a shallow notch in the stone. The idea was that if anyone started messing around with the camouflage, it would spring back at them."

"J.B. told you this?" Grenby asked.

"No. But after I talked him into untying me, and we'd left the cave, he seemed to be taking a lot of time and effort doing something at the mouth of the cave that he didn't want me to see. And puffing and blowing as if it were fairly heavy going. I didn't think of that again until I went up there this afternoon during the memorial service."

"And you discovered something that Mike and his men missed, is that right, Goodey?" Fischer asked. He wanted to get back into the act, even if it was only as the straight man. And he didn't mind calling attention to Grenby's lack of efficiency, either.

"That they'd missed so far," I said modestly. "Tomorrow they'd probably have discovered a long, whip-like branch on the pine beside the mouth of the cave. It's about as thick as my wrist and almost without foliage from being pulled about. J.B. apparently got a bit careless with the trap, and it caught him. The blow was hard enough to turn him and send him reeling over the edge of the cliff." Emma stiffened and recoiled from my words. I felt a tinge of guilt, as if my words had killed him. Fresh pain invaded her face, shattering the stoic calm she'd shown so far.

Instinctively, most of the members of the circle moved toward Emma to comfort her, Hugo in the lead. Nobody had to announce a recess in the megathon. Seeing that Emma was surrounded, Grenby came over to me. I wondered if I looked as silly in that white robe as he did. I led him through a pair of double doors to a small balcony overlooking the misty sea.

"You should have told me earlier, Goodey," he said with a baleful expression on his clean-cut face.

"I didn't get a chance," I said. "Don't be ungrateful. I would have told Dominguez while he was here, but you wouldn't have liked that much. Besides, this way you get all the credit. You said Dominguez wanted results. Besides, think of the hell you can give Shearer for not finding that booby trap. You'll have him under your thumb for life."

A shadow of uncertainty passed over Grenby's features. "Goodey," he said, "are you sure about this? Are you positive it was the limb? You couldn't be wrong?"

"I could be," I said, "but I'm not. It's all there. The limb with dried blood near the business end and even a few of the old man's hairs. Everything but fingerprints. I didn't touch it, but when you bend that limb back to the cave, you'll find that its end will fit neatly into a notch J.B. chiseled into the rock. If you like, I'll take you up there right now and show you."

"No," he said. "Tomorrow morning will be soon enough. What made you suspect a booby trap?"

"I didn't—at first. I thought one of Fischer's not-so-reformed dopers clubbed J.B. and put him over the cliff. But then I saw the notch. J.B. did a neat job, a bit too neat to blame on nature. And I looked for something that might have fitted into it. This could have made a very nice murder. The branch that clubbed J.B. disappeared completely into the foliage."

"I underestimated you, Goodey," Grenby said, a bit ruefully.

"That's all right," I said. "Most people do, and they're usually right." I glanced through the doors to where Hugo and the others were comforting Emma. The break had become more or less official, and coffee had appeared from someplace.

"Tell me, Grenby," I said cautiously, keeping my voice

low, "now that I've figured out how J. B. Carter died, would you say that you trusted me a bit more?"

He thought for a moment, probably wondering what hook I had hidden in that question, then said, reluctantly, "I suppose so. Why?"

"When this megathon starts rolling again," I said, "do you know what's going to happen?"

"No," he said. "I can't say that I do. It's been full of surprises so far." He gave me a look that said he was talking about my encounter with Genie. I don't think he approved.

"I do," I said. "If you'll back my play, I'm going to try to find out who killed Katie Pierce."

"That again?" he said, his look putting me back among the loonies.

"Yes, that again." I was getting tired of his skepticism. "Look," I said, "was I right about J.B.?"

"Yes," he said reluctantly. "I suppose so, but..."

"No buts. I was right. And I've done you a lot of good. You owe me something for that." I added: "Would you rather I asked Dominguez to back me?"

He didn't have to answer that. He wanted me to do that about as much as he wanted bleeding piles. "Look, Goodey," he said, in a reasonable tone of voice, "what's the point of beating a dead horse? I keep telling you that the Pierce case is a dead issue."

"So you keep saying. Crenshaw doesn't think so. Neither do I. We're probably going to be up all night playing Fischer's silly games, anyway, so why shouldn't we play my game for a few minutes? Nobody's got a thing to lose, except the murderer, if there is one. If I'm wrong, nobody loses, and maybe Crenshaw is satisfied. He looks like he's weakening a bit already. Everybody goes home happy. Even me. I get paid whether I succeed or not." I didn't mention the money Emma Carter had promised me. I wondered whether she would pay it.

"All right," said Grenby, more out of weariness than conviction. "What do you want me to do?"

I told him, and the tiredness in his face was replaced with an expression of sheer outrage. "No," he almost shouted. "You're crazy, Goodey. And I don't want anything to do with you. Christ!" He turned to walk back into the room, but I grabbed his arm. Grenby tried to wrench away, but I dug in and got a good grip.

"Listen to me, Grenby," I said. "You haven't any choice. You do as I say or I will get Dominguez out of bed right now and screw you up for fair. And I'll tell him about my little scheme. He'd support me, and you know it. You make a decision right now. Do I make that telephone call?" Grenby wasn't pulling away anymore, so I let go of his arm. He was staring at me with a combination of incredulity and disgust. I wouldn't be invited to his birthday party. I had the feeling that he was going to tell me to telephone Dominguez and be damned.

Before he could, I said: "Grenby, you may not look very much like it right now, but you're still a policeman. To you, Fischer may be the reincarnation of Jesus H. Christ, but you still get paid by the Sheriff's Department of Monterey County. You can turn in your badge in the morning, but right now you're still the law. You can at least help me do your job."

I don't know which part of that harangue got him, but Grenby kept his eyes nailed to mine and said: "You're a son of a bitch, Goodey, but I'll do it. God help you—and me—if you're wrong. Which you are. God help us if you're right, too." He did an about-face and stomped back into the room.

I followed him, hoping that he would keep his promise.

19

"WELL, MIKE," FISCHER SAID, GLOWERING AT GRENBY, "now you can tell Dominguez to go tie a knot in his tail, right? And to stay the hell away from The Institute."

Fischer was full of bonhomie. He'd reconvened the megathon and was back in the catbird seat. Emma had left the room, I imagined to nurse her grief in private. Lenore had returned with Genie, who perched warily next to Pops as if expecting any minute to be throttled. But Pops seemed hardly to realize that she was there, or that any of us were, for that matter.

"I suppose so, Hugo," Grenby said, without much enthusiasm.

"What's the matter, boy?" Fischer asked good-humoredly, "You're not sulking because Goodey found out how J.B. died, are you?"

"No, it's not that," Grenby said, and I was afraid that he'd go on to spill the beans. But Fischer didn't give him a chance.

"Don't worry, Mike," he said. "I'm sure that Goodey won't be greedy with the credit." Fischer looked over at me.

"Will you, Goodey? You wouldn't be a glory hog, would you? Our friend Fred Crenshaw must be paying you pretty well for conducting his wild-goose chase. Isn't that right, Fred?"

This was the first time that Fischer had acknowledged that Crenshaw was alive, much less sitting across the room. Crenshaw seemed to be profoundly disturbed and bemused by the events of the megathon so far. He started to respond to Fischer's question when I cut him off.

"No, I don't mind, Mr. Fischer," I said. "Grenby can have all *that* credit." I saw Grenby tighten his jaw as I went on. "I'm going to be busy taking bows for solving the murder of Katie Pierce."

Perhaps it was the emotional overkill of the megathon so far, but my bombshell, instead of exploding, turned over on its side and quickly sank beneath the surface of a deep and nearly universal indifference. Only Fred Crenshaw seemed very interested, and he gave me a look that I couldn't quite decipher.

Fischer laughed indulgently, obviously dealing with the village idiot. "Are you still beating that old drum?" He turned toward Crenshaw. "Honestly, Fred, you've got to stop sending these sleuths down here to waste my time."

"You didn't understand me, Mr. Fischer," I said, loud enough to guarantee his attention. "I'm saying that I know who killed Katie Pierce. You did." I didn't do anything corny like point a bony finger at him.

That woke him up. Even Pops came out of his funk and reacted as though I'd set his robe on fire. But it was Don Moffitt who looked as though he wanted to break me in half like a wishbone. Fischer said nothing, just put on an offended expression and sat back in mute appeal at my effrontery.

After a sharp intake of breath, the true believers came after in full cry, their voices overlapping in a barrage of abuse that labeled me at least a son of a bitch and probably a Communist spy. The uproar was still growing when a sound cut across it like a bullwhip.

"Shut up! Shut up! All of you. Now, listen to me."

It was Mike Grenby, and from the swollen redness around his gills, he was deadly serious. I'd been wondering when he would make his play. Under the last of his voice, the babble died quickly, and all eyes turned toward Grenby. Especially Fischer's. His bushy eyebrows were flying high.

Once Grenby had everybody's attention, he looked a bit embarrassed and uncertain, but he plowed on. A promise was a promise. "I don't have to remind you," he told them, "that the file on Katie's death is still open. Now, this man has made a serious—if incredible—accusation. He must be heard. So, just shut up and listen. All right, Goodey," he told me. "You've accused Hugo of murder. Back it up." Most of the rest looked tame enough for the moment, but Fischer was giving Grenby a look that wanted handling with asbestos gloves. His expression suggested that Grenby was very close to being a traitor. Now that I had the floor, I had to do something, even if I ended up flat on it.

"To begin with," I told Fischer, "I have J. B. Carter's statement that he saw you push Katie Pierce from the terrace of this building."

That set off another brush fire, but Fischer put it out with a sharp gesture. "Be quiet, all of you," he said, without taking his eyes from my face. They were extraordinary eyes when applied like that. I had an uneasy feeling that they were reading my mind. It was as if Fischer sensed what I was up to, yet was letting me go on. That was interesting in itself.

"Go ahead, Goodey," he said. "Tell us all about it."

"As you know," I said, "from the cliff up there in front of J.B.'s cave, he could look down on the terrace at the seaward side of the building." I felt more like a student giving an oral report to a stern teacher than a man making an accusation of murder. Fischer nodded curtly as if to say: Get on with it, boy.

"J.B.'s eyesight wasn't so sharp, but he had a pretty good pair of binoculars, which he used to spy on you people down here."

"The nosy old bastard," said Moffitt, but Fischer stifled him with a glance.

"Last night," I went on, "J.B. told me that at just about midnight on last December 20th he'd been having a last peep at the mansion before going to bed when he saw you and Katie come out onto the terrace. That was enough to make him stick around a while and watch, despite the bitter cold."

It was enough, too, to make Fred Crenshaw turn toward Fischer with a look of keen, if ambiguous, interest. I don't know if I was convincing anyone, but I had their attention. Even Grenby had lost some of his doubtful look.

"J.B. said that for some time you seemed to be doing most of the talking, and Katie was just listening, almost as if you had her hypnotized," I told Fischer. "But then Katie suddenly stopped listening and started doing the talking—or, more likely, shouting. J.B. said it looked to him as if she were getting a bit hysterical, and then she shoved you away from her and ran toward the front of the terrace toward the sea."

Everyone was listening now, like small children hearing a fairy tale. I forged on before I lost them.

"By this time," I said, "Katie was at the edge of the

terrace, with you right behind her. You sprang toward her and then..."

"Stop!"

It was a hell of a loud shout for such an apparently frail old man, and it stopped me cold. Pops Martin was on his feet looking like the ghost of Jimmy Cagney. His creased old face was straining at the seams, and he was trying to get my attention. The revolver in his right hand told me that. It was the same .38 police special I'd handed over to Fischer for safekeeping. And he had it pointed at me in a very determined manner. How he got it out of his flowing robes, I'll never know.

"If you say another word, I'll blow your fucking head off," he said. I believed him.

Mike Grenby was on his way to his feet when Pops turned in his direction. Genie had her head down and was trying to crawl under her cushion.

"Sit down, Mike," Pops ordered, "and you won't get hurt." Grenby eased himself back down with wary grace. "You," Pops said, giving me all his attention, "you think you're pretty smart, don't you?"

I know a rhetorical question when I hear one, so I kept my mouth shut. I allowed myself a slight shrug just so he wouldn't think I was being unresponsive.

"Well, you're not," Pops said to nobody's surprise "You're so dumb you make me sick. If you think—if you think this man," he said, turning to look toward Fischer but keeping me under the gun, "could—"

Pops was getting choked up, and the hand holding my gun was none too steady. He took a deep breath and started again. "If you think this man could kill anyone—could kill a young girl—you're just—just—oh, damn you!" he nearly sobbed, raising the revolver and putting the sight between my eyes. "You fucking..."

"Pops," said Fischer quietly, but he didn't move.

Pops closed his pale eyes tightly as if trying to concentrate. His flaccid old chops went rigid from the strain. I thought about rushing him, but then his eyes opened again.

"I don't care what that loony old bastard said he saw," Pops went on. "He didn't see Hugo on the terrace with Katie that night. It was me!"

"Pops," Hugo said warningly. "Don't—"

The old man gestured with his free hand. "Don't worry, Hugo," he said. "It's okay. I've got to do it. I'm just sorry that —" He put his hand to his forehead. "I'm sorry, Hugo, I really am. I—"

"All right, old fellow," Fischer said soothingly. "Take it easy."

"I've got to tell it, Hugo," Pops continued. "I have to. I've been wanting to get this off my chest since—but now— I've got to tell it. I want you to know the truth." Pops was talking to Fischer, but the gun told me that I hadn't been forgotten.

"Go ahead then, Pops," Fischer said. "Tell it the way it happened. Take your time." Fischer didn't seem to mind that the revolver was pointed at my sternum, and I didn't like to mention it. Pops turned back toward me with an angry face. "Don't think you've got any credit coming, Goodey," he said. "I would have had to cop out eventually. I couldn't have held my mud forever. Not on something like this. Listen," he said loudly, glaring around the room. "I want to make it clear that I didn't murder anybody. Nobody!" He gave me a hard squint as if I were going to argue with him. No chance.

Pops put his hand to his forehead again. His face was

flushed with exertion. "Let me tell it just exactly like it happened," he said, almost pleading.

I was beginning to wonder if he ever would—before he shot me, that is.

"I admit that I was hot for Katie," Pops told us. "A lot of guys were." He gave Mark Kinsey a look. "And she liked me, I know she did. But then things began to go wrong just after I asked her to marry me. She began to pull away from me, said she had to have more time to decide. Then she started hanging around more with that asshole Verrein. I got rid of him," he said with some pride, "but things still weren't right. It was almost as if she was running from me. I couldn't even talk to her. But I tried. Christ, I loved her.

"Finally," he went on, "that night—it was after the Saturday night open house—I caught up with Katie. I had to have it out with her. I was going nuts. At last, she said she'd talk to me. That's all I wanted to do—talk to her. Honest to God! After the guests left, we came up the stairs to the terrace. It was freezing out, so we had our heavy coats on. Maybe that's why J.B. thought it was Hugo, but it wasn't. It was me!"

He shouted this last part at me, and I wasn't going to disagree with him. It didn't look like Fred Crenshaw was, either. He was watching Pops with more pity than anger on his face.

"Anyway," Pops continued, "Katie was very quiet, but I figured maybe she was just thinking. I don't know what I thought. I was just trying to tell her that I loved her, that she shouldn't be afraid of me. She wasn't arguing, so I thought maybe..."

Pops' face had been almost calm, but there was pain in it as he went on. "But then she turned on me, real nasty like, and said: 'All right, old man, what do you want?' And suddenly, in the bright moonlight, I got a look at her eyes. Katie was loaded. Absolutely. Christ, I didn't even suspect, and I can smell a doper a mile away. I didn't know what she was using, but it was really messing with her mind. I only wanted—honest—" He shot a look at Fischer, "to get her off that damned terrace. I reached out to grab her, but she got scared and started running away from me. She was like a goddamned moth flitting all over the place."

He stopped for a moment and looked at Fred Crenshaw. "On my life," he said, "I didn't know what to do. I know now that I should have left her and got help, but—I said, 'Katie, now be sensible, Katie. Let's go downstairs.' But she wouldn't listen. Every time I took a step toward her, she backed away, getting wilder by the second. I stopped, but she kept backing toward the edge. Suddenly, she was right at the edge of the terrace, and she started to fall. She must have tripped. I reached out to grab for her, to pull her back. I got her coat, but she was twisting—she ripped right out of my hands—" his voice dropped—"and she was gone. Gone. She didn't make a sound. It was so dark below, I couldn't— she was gone."

Pops stopped, looked at Fred Crenshaw and then at Fischer. "God, Hugo," he said softly, "I'm so sorry—so..."As if with a will of its own, the revolver swung up in his hand until his arm was doubled, and the barrel was pointed toward his head. With a jerky motion, Pops shoved the muzzle into his mouth, closed his eyes and pulled the trigger.

The snap of the hammer striking the empty chamber wasn't loud, but it was the loudest sound in that room. Before Pops could pull the trigger again—if he'd planned to —Mike Grenby was up on his feet and had taken the revolver from his hand. Pops didn't resist, just opened his eyes with surprise at finding himself still alive. I was glad that my first weapons instructor had advised me to always keep one empty chamber. Nobody likes to get splattered with blood, brains and bits of skull bone.

Pops collapsed like a tired, old balloon, and Grenby had to catch him to keep him from falling. "Help Pops to his cushion, Mike," Fischer said gently.

"Give Goodey his gun, Mike," Fischer said after Pops had been resettled. "He's leaving now."

I took my revolver. There didn't seem to be any place for it in my flowing robes, so I just let it dangle gracefully from one hand.

Fischer turned from me as if I'd just vanished. "Well, Fred," he said almost conversationally, "you've got what you wanted. We're in your hands. You can destroy The Institute now—if that's what you want to do."

He paused as if expecting an answer, but Crenshaw looked as though he were having too much trouble dealing with recent revelations to know how to respond. Fortunately, Fischer didn't mind taking up the slack.

"Yes," he went on, "all you've got to do is tell Dominguez what you've heard in this room tonight, and we might as well close up our doors for good. Pops will most likely die in prison, and I wouldn't be surprised if I ended up there, too. Fortunately," he added dryly, "I've been in prison before, so it won't be much of a hardship. But it will be a hardship to many of my people if you throw them out on the street before they're ready. Many will die. Is that what you want, Fred?"

"No, but..."

"You have every right to want somebody to pay for the senseless death of your granddaughter. I believe in vengeance. And if that's what you want, I'm your man." He held up his hands as if ready for the nails.

I was willing to go get Crenshaw a hammer, but his troubled expression said that he was too busy dealing with the unexpected.

"It's not easy to admit," Fischer went on, "but we failed Katie. I failed her." Protests bubbled up around the circle, but Fischer wasn't in the mood to share Crenshaw's attention. "It's true," he said strongly, "and it's about the greatest tragedy we've had here at The Institute. I'm going to do my best to see that it doesn't happen to some other child. But you can do a lot more than I to make sure of that."

That roused Crenshaw from his trance, all right, and it interested me, too. I was watching Fischer as a batter does a good junk-ball pitcher, just to see what he'd come up with next. This was a change-up neither Crenshaw nor I had expected.

"Oh, I don't mean whether or not you blow the whistle to Dominguez," Fischer continued. "I'm talking about what you decide to do with the three million dollars Katie left The Institute in her will."

"You know about that?" Crenshaw managed, but it was an ordeal.

"Of course," Fischer said modestly. "Did you think I wouldn't?"

"But nobody's ever said..." Crenshaw began in a puzzled voice.

"No, and we never would have. As much as The Institute needs money, we wouldn't want to get it that way." Crenshaw looked as though he might want to believe Fischer, but I had my doubts. "Of course," Fischer said, "my lawyers could bump heads with yours for a few years, and we might end up with some of the crumbs they leave, but that will never happen. Whether or not Katie wanted us to have her money, Fred, it's all yours. We'll never bring that will to the light of day."

To my coarse ear, this sounded like a bribe, but Crenshaw didn't seem to be taking it that way. Fischer's words seemed to sink into him without a trace. I couldn't have told you what he was thinking.

"But," Fischer said, "I don't mind telling you what we could have done with that money, Fred." Here it comes, I thought, the old curve ball. "We could have started a whole new facet of The Institute, a program specifically for troubled youngsters like Katie. So that boys and girls like her would get the special care they need." Fischer had Crenshaw's whole attention then, and he dropped the bomb. "And I think it would have been fitting to have named that program after Katie's father. He was Frederick M. Crenshaw, Jr., wasn't he, Fred?"

Fischer had to ask that like I needed to be reminded that Aristotle was a Greek. This was all getting a bit strong for me. "Wait a minute, Mr. Crenshaw," I said. "Don't let his..."

Fischer turned his great head back toward me. "Get out of here, Goodey," he said flatly. "You've done what you came here to do."

"Not quite, Mr. Fischer," I said. "There is the little matter of where Katie Pierce got the barbiturates. Or don't you think that's important?"

Before Fischer could answer, a voice came from a completely unexpected quarter: "I don't think that matters very much anymore, Goodey," said Fred Crenshaw. "Go back to San Francisco. I'll send you a check for the rest of your fee."

"Doesn't matter?" I asked. "Sure it matters. Pops would never have chased Katie off the terrace if she hadn't been high on barbiturates. She got them here in this haven of mental health and clean living, and I can prove it. The pills that killed your granddaughter, Mr. Crenshaw, came from James Carey," I said, pointing at him, "this wonderful organization's own Dr. Feelgood."

I don't know who was more surprised—Fischer or Carey.

"Jim," demanded Fischer angrily, "is there any truth in what he says?"

"No!" Carey's flush of indignation was genuine. "For Christ's sake, Hugo. You know I'd never have given Katie—"

"I didn't say you gave the pills to Katie," I cut in. "I just said that they came from you—by way of Tommy Carter."

The truth has a ring to it that can't be ignored. It was as if I'd snapped my fingernail against the lip of a fine crystal goblet. "The fact is, Carey," I said, pursuing my advantage, "that you have been keeping Tommy manageable by judicious—if not widely publicized—doses of barbiturates, isn't that so?"

"There's nothing illegal about that," Carey shot back, "I'm Tommy's doctor. I—"

"No, not illegal, Carey," I said, "but it made it easy for Katie—when the pressure Pops was putting on her got too intense—to wheedle a bit of painkiller out of Tommy." I turned back to Crenshaw. "I think that's about all you'll need, Mr. Crenshaw," I said. "Whether or not Grenby can bring himself to put the county's interests before The Institute's wellbeing, I don't know, but I don't think you'll have any trouble with them."

"I told you before that it doesn't matter, Goodey," Crenshaw said. "You can go now."

I got the distinct impression that I was being dismissed. Crenshaw was less than embarrassing with his gratitude, but that's one thing a cop learns to live without. "All right," I said. "Nice working for you." Nobody stood in my way, but before I could get through the door, Crenshaw said something that stopped me like a sheet of plate glass.

"Hugo," I heard him say, "there is something I have to explain to you about the money due to you from Katie's estate."

I spun faster than the average tight end. "You what?" I said, none too quietly.

"I'm going to tell them what I've done with the three million dollars," Crenshaw told me in a none-of-your-business tone of voice. He turned back toward Fischer as if I'd just left the room. "I—"

"Wait a minute," I insisted. "Just hold on." Crenshaw turned toward me, but he didn't do it gladly.

"After all you've learned here tonight about Katie's death," I said, "you're going to—" Then it dawned on me. "Hell, you're going to give them that money, aren't you, Mr. Crenshaw? With all that I found out for you, one of your good, crooked lawyers could tie that estate up for decades. But you, you're going to make them a gift of it, aren't you. I've just been wasting my time here."

"You'll be paid in full," Crenshaw said coldly. "The rest of it is none—"

"Christ!" I said. "You've fallen for Fischer's bullshit, too." I shook my head. "Mr. Crenshaw—"

Fischer cut in. "Jack—" Gillette materialized at my side. "Please show Mr. Goodey to his room to change and then escort him to his automobile." There was triumph in his voice.

Gillette moved through the open doorway and waited for me to follow. But I wasn't quite ready. "Wait," I said, and I turned back so that I could take in the entire group. They sat there in an unbroken circle, and I was on the outside. I noticed that one of the flunkies had even removed my cushion. Rachel and Aileen Moffitt had shifted closer together to fill the gap. Their eyes were turned in my direction, but nobody saw me. They were just waiting for the door to close. I couldn't think of a thing to say.

"Fuck it," I said, and walked through the doorway. With the click of it shutting, I heard Fischer's voice, faintly but distinctly, begin to welcome Crenshaw to the fold.

20

GILLETTE WAS WALKING HALF A STEP BEHIND MY right shoulder, ostentatiously just seeing me off the premises.

"You know, Jack," I said chummily, "for a man who did what he came here to do and accidentally figured out how J.B. died, somehow I don't feel like a winner."

"You're not," he said. "You never had a chance."

"How do you figure it?" I asked. "How could Crenshaw fall for Fischer's bullshit—after all he's seen here?" Then it occurred to me that perhaps Gillette wasn't the best person to ask. "Sorry. I mean, it could cost him at least three million dollars and probably a lot more."

"The money doesn't seem to have done a lot for him so far," Gillette said. "Your guess is as good as mine. Everybody comes here for something different. Don't overwork your brain." We were walking up the broad staircase. "You're not going to be around long enough to worry about it."

He was right, but I couldn't help wondering. Gillette waited in the doorway while I removed the flowing white robe. "I can't say it hasn't been a weekend full of surprises," I said as I dressed. "There have been very few really dull moments."

"We like to keep things lively."

"By the way," I said, tying my shoelaces, "I didn't get a chance to thank you for getting me out of the sauna."

"No problem," he said. "I'm just sorry that I had to give Tommy a thick ear."

"I'm not sorry," I said. "As a figure of harmless fun, Tommy Carter leaves a lot to be desired."

"He's okay. Tommy's just that little bit too eager to follow suggestions from a good friend. An old, good friend like Pops who—" Gillette looked at me sharply. "Hey, I'm not telling you anything you don't know, am I?"

"Of course not," I lied. "But maybe I ought to go tie a knot in that old bastard's tail." I stepped toward the door.

"Maybe you'd better not," said Gillette, filling the doorway.

"But don't you think I ought to be just a little bit sore?"

"Who at?" asked Gillette. "I told you this was a nut house."

"Yeah. I forgot." I looked around the little room. It no longer contained anything of mine, and I couldn't work up any nostalgia about leaving it. I hadn't had that many good times there.

"Come on," I said to Gillette. "You were supposed to be throwing me out. Remember?"

"Oh, yeah. I nearly forgot."

"How do you figure it will all work out?" I asked him as we walked down the stairs.

"What's that?"

"Well, The Institute is okay on J.B. Grenby can go to town on that one, even if a few nigglers might think it odd that a millionaire had to hide out on his own estate and set booby-traps to ensure his privacy."

"Let 'em wonder," Gillette said. "It's good exercise."

"But Katie Pierce is a different matter," I said. "Whether or not he meant to, Pops did chase her off the roof. And she did get high on drugs provided by Carey. That could be a bit sticky, what with Grenby still wearing the sheriff's uniform and all."

"I don't think so," Gillette said blithely. "Grenby may still be a cop—technically—but he's more Hugo's man than he is Dominguez's. And with Crenshaw not creating any more fuss, Katie's death is going to stay a sad, unexplainable accident."

"And Katie's three million bucks?"

"Hugo will put that to good use," Gillette said. "You can count on that."

"And he'll take Crenshaw along with it?"

"Always room for another old geezer—uh, elder statesman—at The Institute," he said.

"Do you think Fischer will keep his word and start that new program he was selling to Crenshaw?"

"Probably. He's been wanting to do something like that anyway. This way, he can name it after Crenshaw Junior, and everybody will be happy."

"Especially Fischer."

"Especially Hugo," he said. "I believe you're beginning to understand how this place works."

"Just barely," I said. "But what if some use for that money comes up that Fischer thinks is more important? Do you think he might change his mind a little bit?

Gillette cocked his head at me. "I'd better get you out of here before you understand too much." We were then on the second floor landing.

"How about you, Jack?" I asked as we descended. "Do you plan to stay snug in the bosom of St. Hugo?"

"Until something better comes along. If something ever does."

By then we were standing in the marble foyer under Rudy Verrein's majestic portrait of Fischer. Gillette was about to open the door when Rachel Schute came out of the darkness toward us.

"Joe?" she said. She had a piece of paper in her hand. "It's okay, Jack," Rachel said. "You go back to the megathon. I want to say goodbye to—to our guest."

"Okay, Rachel," Gillette said, turning to walk into the darkness.

"So long, Jack," I said, but he either didn't hear me or didn't bother to answer.

"Here," said Rachel, shoving the piece of paper into my hand. "Emma asked me to give you this."

I looked at the check. It had the right number of zeroes. I put it quickly into my pocket. "Thank her for me."

"Do you think you earned it, Joe?"

"Did you earn yours?" I asked, perhaps a bit unkindly. Rachel flushed. That would always be her enemy. "Nobody asked Emma to offer the money," I said. "Do you think she wants it back?"

"No."

"Goodbye, Rachel," I said, turning toward the door.

"Tell me something, Joe," she said as if she hadn't heard me. "Did J.B. really tell you that he'd seen Hugo and Katie on the terrace?"

"Does it matter?"

"It matters to me," she said seriously.

"Can you keep a secret?"

"No," she said, and I knew that she wouldn't.

"J.B. didn't tell me that he'd seen anything on the terrace," I said. "In a careless moment, he did claim that Fischer had killed Katie, but that was just loose talk. I made the rest of it up." I hoped that didn't sound too much like bragging.

For a time, Rachel didn't say anything. She just looked at me with somber eyes, a dark turquoise in the dim light. "Are you proud of yourself, Joe?" she said at last.

"I did the job I was hired to do," I said. "Two jobs."

"Do you think it was worth doing?" She obviously didn't.

"Crenshaw had a right to know how his granddaughter died," I said. "Or don't you think it was important?"

"At what cost, Joe?" she asked. "At what cost? Would you do anything, say anything, just to do a job?"

There was no answer to that question. "I've got a long drive ahead of me, Rachel," I said.

But she wasn't ready to let me go. Not yet.

"Just like that?" she said, her usually soft voice getting shrill. "Don't you even know what you tried to do here tonight? Thank God you failed."

"You tell me."

"You tried to destroy The Institute," she said, "just to solve a murder that never was. Just to earn your blood money, you were willing to destroy all that Hugo has spent over ten years of his life building. Not that you could, of course. It would take a lot bigger man than you could ever be."

"Then what are you complaining about?" I asked. "Goodey has shot his best shot, and The Institute remains in all its monolithic beauty."

"What bothers me, Joe," Rachel said seriously, "is what you tried to do. The despicable methods you used. You were like some digging animal turning up rocks to see what was under them, not caring what harm you might do in the process. For all you cared, all the lives The Institute has saved could have been lost. If Mike Grenby wasn't..."

"In Fischer's pocket?" I said, finishing her sentence in a way that I'm sure Rachel hadn't intended. "Yeah, he could blow this place up with all he learned tonight. It's a good thing for Fischer that Grenby is a good boy who has his priorities right."

Rachel's eyes were full of scorn. "Joe," she began.

"No," I said, deciding that I wasn't too tired to get pissed off, "you've had a good time telling me what a rat I am, Rachel. Now, let me give you my version."

Rachel started to turn away from me, but I got her arm in a strong grip and turned her around. "You just listen," I said, "then you can go back to your playmates." Her eyes said they didn't think much of me, but I let go of her arm anyway. She didn't move.

"All right," I said, "you don't like my methods. But I was pretty sure that if I pushed Fischer hard enough, the right man would surface, especially if he was already carrying a heavy burden of guilt. And I was right, wasn't I?"

"Pops didn't murder..."

"No," I said, "that's just the point. A jury might beg to differ, but Pops wasn't responsible for Katie's death. That responsibility belongs right up there in Hugo Fischer's fat lap."

"You're—"

"Hear me," I said, forcefully enough to make Rachel shut her mouth in a thin line. "The responsibility—and the guilt—has to ride with Fischer because he's set himself up as God around here. He makes the rules and he breaks them if it suits his whim. There are no drugs allowed at The Institute—unless it suits his purpose. The Institute is a haven for disturbed young girls like Katie, unless God's horny old right-hand man decides to prey on them. Everyone must bend to Fischer's grand scheme or get out—even if it's J. B. Carter, and he owns the place. It was just Fischer's bad luck that this combination accidentally cost two lives. But I imagine that he—and the rest of you—figure that is a small price to pay for the survival of The Institute."

I stopped to give Rachel a chance to butt in, but she stood there looking at me with alien eyes. Finally, she asked: "Are you finished?"

"Not quite. I'm not saying that Fischer isn't a pretty good social mechanic with energy—and ego—to burn. In a tin-pot sort of way, he's a real dazzler, and he'll probably go on gathering followers like blue serge picks up lint. Look at the way he bundled up Crenshaw tonight. I still can't believe it. If he wanted to, he could make you True Believers think that night was day and Jesus was a Dutchman."

"You're jealous," Rachel shot, her eyes regaining some of their fire.

"Sure, I'm jealous. If I had some of Fischer's talent, I wouldn't have to do jobs like this one. Jobs where everyone wins but the Katie Pierces and other casualties of The Institute's big meat grinder. Where everything comes out but the truth."

"You could still go to the police yourself," Rachel said.

"Sure I could, but that's not my job. Don't mistake me for a moralist, Rachel. You know better. I'm just an ex-cop scuffling after enough money to stay alive and operating. If some justice gets done in the process, that's fine. It makes the client feel better about paying. But I won't lose much sleep because the truth about Katie Pierce's death will never come out. What is the truth? That she got chewed up and spat out in a minor malfunction of Hugo Fischer's social movement? If Katie Pierce is remembered at all, it will be as a kooky pill head who brought Fred Crenshaw and a lot of money to The Institute. And what about J.B.? He's just a casualty of progress, like the rabbit that gets buried under the concrete of a freeway. Nobody's to blame; it just happened. Who was it that said that you can't make an omelet without breaking eggs? Too true. But just once in a while, Rachel, you might want to take a good, close look at the omelet as you step over the broken eggshells."

I'd said all I had to say, but Rachel didn't respond. She was still standing there when I closed the big door behind me.

It was even darker in the parking lot when I climbed into the Morris, put the key in the ignition and pulled the starter. Nothing. I pulled again. Double nothing. I let my head fall forward and slumped in the seat. Opening my eyes, I thought about trying to push the car to a start. I thought about going back to the mansion and asking to use their telephone to call a garage, but somehow that didn't appeal. I thought about picking the car up and carrying it over my shoulder.

Fishing my suitcase out of the back seat, I gave the fender of the old car a vicious kick and began trudging up the steep drive. About half way up to the tree line, I looked back at the mansion. One light at a corner of the big building was ablaze, and I tried to imagine what was happening in that room. It was too much work.

I didn't know what had happened to the security guards, but there was nobody manning the mined barrier. It was just as well; we probably wouldn't have had much to say to each other. When I got to the highway, I crossed over to the northbound lane. I sat my suitcase down, put what I hoped was a confidence-inspiring expression on my face and stuck out my right thumb just as a set of high beams came barreling out of a turn about a hundred yards down the road.

Blinded by the light, nearly deafened by the roar of too much horsepower, I listened hopefully for the screech of tires. I didn't hear it. When vision returned to my light-saturated eyes, all I could see was two ruby taillights doing their best to disappear in the first faint shadows of dawn.

I turned around and stuck my thumb out again. It was going to be a long morning.

THE END

ABOUT THE AUTHOR

Charles Alverson's writing career has spanned over five decades, during which he has written for publications such as *The Wall Street Journal*, *Rolling Stone*, and *HELP! Magazine*. Alverson has written ten novels, two children's books, and helped co-write the screenplays for Terry Gilliam's cult films *Jabberwocky* and *Brazil*.

Alverson currently lives in Serbia, where he has resided with his wife since 1994.

Download Alverson's anthology of short fiction *Ryan's Way & Other Short Stories* when you sign up for his free author newsletter at watchfirepress.com/alverson.